THE BOOKBINDER'S ORPHAN DAUGHTER

DOROTHY WELLINGS

CORNERSTONETALES.COM

1
NEEDLES, LEATHER, AND POETRY

WINTER, 1843

Dust motes danced in the golden shafts of morning light that spilled through the workshop windows. Eleven-year-old Meredith traced her fingers along the spines of newly bound volumes. The wooden shelves creaked beneath the weight of countless stories, their leather bindings gleaming in various shades of burgundy, forest green, and deep blue.

Thomas Aldrich's tools hung in precise rows against the far wall – brass finishing wheels catching glints of sunlight, awls and needles arranged by size, each implement waiting for the next day's work. The polished workbench dominated the centre of the room, its surface marked by years of careful craftsmanship and bearing the subtle indentations of countless hours spent binding precious volumes.

Between the shelves, narrow aisles created a maze of literary treasures. Some books stood proud and tall, while others huddled together, their spines weathered by time and handling. The morning sun painted patterns across the wooden floorboards, highlighting the worn paths where her father paced as he worked.

Meredith closed her eyes and drew in a deep breath. The familiar scent of leather and glue filled her lungs – a complex aroma that spoke of dedication and artistry. Beneath it lay subtler notes: the mustiness of old paper, the sharp tang of brass polish, the earthiness of wood. These smells had become the very essence of home, weaving themselves into her earliest memories.

Outside, London stirred to life. Cart wheels clattered against cobblestones, and voices from Cedar's Printing House next door filtered through the walls. The smell of fresh bread wafted in from Mrs Cooper's Bakery, mingling with the workshop's own distinct perfume. Yet within these walls, time seemed to slow, creating a peaceful haven from the city's chaos.

Meredith gripped the awl with practiced care, her small fingers finding their familiar position on the worn wooden handle. The leather-bound volume before her waited, its signatures arranged in perfect alignment. She drew in a measured breath, steadying her hand.

Her father worked at the opposite end of the bench, his movements fluid and precise as he stretched deep burgundy Moroccan leather across the boards of a first edition. His weathered hands moved with certainty born from decades of experience, each gesture purposeful and measured.

The awl pierced the thick paper with a satisfying whisper. Meredith guided it through the fold, creating perfect holes at exact intervals. Her father had taught her to feel the rhythm of the work – too close together and the binding would weaken, too far apart and the pages would gap. The stack of signatures beside her grew smaller as she progressed, each one receiving the same careful attention.

She paused between sections, stealing glances at her father's technique. Thomas's fingers danced across the leather, smoothing away air bubbles and ensuring perfect contact with the board beneath. A thin sheen of paste glistened on the material's underside, catching the morning light. His movements held a grace that Meredith hoped to one day achieve – the kind that made difficult work appear effortless.

Her dark hair fell forward, and she tucked it behind her ear with her free hand, leaving a small smudge of glue on her cheek. The awl moved steadily through the next signature, creating another row of precise holes ready for binding.

She looked up again, studying how her father's hands applied just the right pressure to work the leather into the spine's curves. His fingers knew exactly where to press, how to coax the material into embracing the book's form. Meredith's heart swelled with pride as she watched him work, determined to absorb every detail of his mastery.

In the corner, her mother's voice rose and fell like gentle waves. Elizabeth sat in her cherished armchair, the one with roses and vines that had faded into soft whispers of their original vibrancy. Sunlight caught the silver threads in her light brown hair, creating a halo effect that made Meredith's heart squeeze with love.

The leather-bound volume rested in Elizabeth's lap, its pages spread wide beneath her delicate fingers. Her blue eyes danced across the text, bringing Shakespeare's words to life with each carefully crafted phrase. Her alto voice filled every corner of the workshop, wrapping around the tools and books like a warm embrace.

"'What's in a name? That which we call a rose by any other name would smell as sweet.'" Elizabeth's voice carried Romeo's longing, each word precise and measured. She paused, letting the poetry settle in the air between the leather and glue.

Elizabeth shifted in her chair, the worn fabric creaking softly beneath her. The morning light caught the silver locket at her throat, the one containing the miniature picture from her wedding day. Her fingers traced the page's edge with reverence before continuing, her voice rising and falling with the rhythm of the verse.

Meredith's fingers paused on the awl as her mother painted pictures in the morning air. Elizabeth's words transformed the workshop into a Verona street, where star-crossed lovers exchanged promises beneath a moonlit balcony. Her familiar surroundings melded with imagined Italian gardens, creating a world that existed between the reality of their modest workshop and the boundless realm of Shakespeare's creation.

Her mother's silver locket caught the light as she leaned forward, each word precise and measured. The way Elizabeth's fingers traced the pages, treating each leaf with the same care Thomas showed his finest leather bindings, made Meredith's chest tighten with love.

"'Deny thy father and refuse thy name,'" Elizabeth's voice swelled with emotion, her blue eyes dancing across the text. "'Or, if thou wilt not, be but sworn my love, and I'll no longer be a Capulet.'"

Thomas looked up from his work, burgundy leather forgotten beneath his skilled hands. His eyes met Elizabeth's across the workshop, and something passed between them – a current of understanding that made the air itself seem to shimmer. The corner of his mouth lifted in a tender smile, and Elizabeth's voice grew softer, more intimate, as if the words were meant for him alone.

Meredith watched their exchange, her own heart full. The

way her mother brought stories to life, the careful attention her father paid to each binding – these were the threads that wove their family together. She imagined herself someday, reading to children of her own, passing on not just the words but the magic that lived within them.

Elizabeth's voice carried on, steady and clear as a bell, each syllable perfectly formed. Meredith's hands resumed their work, but her mind danced with the poetry, storing away her mother's cadence and inflection like precious treasures.

The awl slipped. Sharp pain shot through Meredith's finger, and a bright bead of blood welled up against her skin. She bit her lip, trapping the gasp in her throat. The perfect line of holes in the signature blurred as tears pricked her eyes.

Thomas's workbench creaked as he set down his tools. His footsteps crossed the workshop floor, and his warm hand settled on her shoulder. "Let me see."

Meredith held out her trembling finger. The drop of blood had grown larger, threatening to fall onto the pristine paper below. Her father's weathered hands cupped her smaller one, turning it in the morning light.

"The awl found you, did it?" Thomas reached for the small medical kit they kept near the washing basin. "Every bookbinder pays for their craft in blood at some point."

Elizabeth set aside Romeo and Juliet, the poetry forgotten as she rose from her chair. Her skirts rustled as she crossed to Meredith's side. "Your father speaks true. I've bandaged his fingers more times than I can count."

Thomas cleaned the small wound with practiced movements. "The first time I used an awl, I managed to stick myself three times in one afternoon." He wrapped a strip of clean linen around her finger with gentle precision. "Each scar is a lesson learned."

Elizabeth's cool hand brushed Meredith's cheek. "There now. No lasting harm done."

The bandage was snug but not too tight, much like the bindings her father created. Meredith flexed her finger, testing the wrap. The sting had already begun to fade, replaced by a dull throb that matched her heartbeat.

"Thank you," she whispered, looking up at her parents' concerned faces. Their love wrapped around her like the finest Morocco leather, protective and precious.

SHADOWS CREPT across the workshop floor as afternoon light filtered through the windows. Meredith set down her tools and stretched her tired fingers, the small bandage catching on the edge of her sleeve. Around her, leather-bound volumes stood like silent sentinels on the shelves her father had built by hand. Each book held not just its printed story, but the tale of its creation – the careful selection of materials, the precise stitching, the loving attention to every detail.

Her fingertips traced the gold lettering on a nearby spine. The workshop felt alive with possibility, even in the growing dimness. One day, she'd have her own space like this, she decided. A place where she could experiment with new binding techniques, perhaps even create entirely new styles of covers that no one had attempted before.

The clatter of hooves against cobblestones drifted through the open window, accompanied by a chorus of street vendors hawking their wares. Children's laughter rang out — probably the Baker twins chasing each other again, she thought. But inside the workshop, time moved differently.

Meredith breathed deeply, taking in the familiar smells that meant home. This was their sanctuary – every tool hanging in its proper place, every shelf loaded with stories waiting to be bound or mended. Even the worn floorboards beneath her feet felt sacred, marked by years of careful footsteps and dropped threads.

She ran her hand along the smooth surface of her father's workbench, feeling the slight indentations that told the story of countless books brought to life under his skilled hands. The workshop was more than just a place of business – it was the heart of their family, beating steady and strong against the rhythm of London's streets.

Thomas pressed the final gilt letters into the leather spine. The first edition gleamed in the late afternoon light, its burgundy surface catching golden highlights from the workshop windows. Meredith leaned forward, drinking in every detail of the finished work – the perfectly squared corners, the delicate headbands, the precise alignment of the text block.

"Come here, little one." Thomas beckoned her closer, his weathered hands still bearing traces of gold leaf. "See how the spine flexes? That's the mark of proper binding. Each signature we sewed, every station we marked – they all serve a purpose."

Elizabeth set aside her worn copy of Romeo and Juliet, her eyes bright with maternal pride as she watched them. "You've learned so quickly, darling."

"Your mother's right." Thomas ran his finger along the smooth edge of the cover. "Never forget that every task matters, whether it's making those first holes with the awl or finishing the finest leather. Each step builds upon the last, like verses in a poem."

Meredith's heart swelled as she studied their shared handiwork. The book represented more than just bound pages — it was a testament to their family's dedication to craft. She thought of all the readers who would hold this volume, fingers tracing the same gilt letters she'd watched her father press into place. Their workshop might be small, tucked away on Paternoster Row, but their work would travel far beyond these walls.

Her fingertip brushed against the small bandage, a reminder of her earlier mishap. But now, instead of feeling clumsy, she felt marked — initiated into a legacy of craftspeople who had pricked their fingers and stained their hands in service of binding stories together.

"Thank you," she whispered, though the words felt inadequate to express the depth of her gratitude. This was more than just learning a trade – it was finding her place in a tradition that stretched back generations, each book a bridge between past and future.

2

WORTHY OF THEIR WORDS

Meredith pulled the small leather journal from beneath her workbench, its cover still fresh with the scent of glue and leather. She'd bound it herself last week, using scraps from her father's cuttings – a patchwork of different textures that created an abstract pattern across the surface. Her fingers felt the uneven edges where she'd joined the pieces together.

The blank pages beckoned. She dipped her pen in ink and began to write, creating a tale of a young apprentice who discovered magical properties in the leather she used for binding. The words flowed easier than she'd expected, her imagination sparked by years of listening to her mother's readings.

Elizabeth's voice rose and fell as she read from Much Ado About Nothing, her hands painting pictures in the air. Each gesture brought the words to life in a way that mere reading never could.

Turning back to her journal, Meredith tried to capture that same sense of movement in her writing. She described how her character's hands trembled as she discovered the first enchanted binding, the way the leather seemed to pulse with hidden energy. The ink smudged slightly where her excitement made her writing hasty, but she didn't mind – it gave the pages character, like the worn edges of her father's favorite books.

Between sentences, she glanced up at Elizabeth, studying how her mother's face reflected each emotion in the text. A soft smile played across Elizabeth's lips during romantic passages, her brow furrowed during moments of tension. Meredith wanted her own words to dance like that, to leap off the page and touch people's hearts the way her mother's readings touched hers.

She bent over her journal again, her pen scratching against the paper as she wove her tale, each word a stitch binding the story together.

Thomas paused his work, setting down the finishing wheel he'd been polishing. His weathered hands, stained with years of working with leather dyes, rested on the workbench.

"Your mother breathes life into those words," he said, nodding toward Elizabeth. "Just as we breathe life into these books." He picked up a finished volume, its burgundy cover gleaming in the afternoon light. "Each story she reads, each book we bind — they're all pieces of who we are."

Meredith's fingers traced the uneven stitching of her journal. The thread wasn't quite as straight as her father's work, but he'd taught her that imperfections gave character to a piece.

"I saw you writing in that journal," Thomas said. His eyes crinkled at the corners. "You've got your mother's gift for words and your old dad's hands for binding. That's a rare combination." He reached for one of his tools, a bone folder passed down from his own father. "You could do something special with that — create books that are beautiful inside and out."

The leather scraps of her journal caught the light, each

piece telling its own story through texture and shade. Thomas ran his finger along the patchwork pattern she'd created.

"See how you've made something new from these different pieces? That's what storytelling is – taking bits and pieces of life and binding them together into something meaningful." He smiled, the same warm smile he gave when she mastered a particularly difficult stitch. "You could write stories that deserve bindings as special as the words inside them."

The muffled voices from Cedar's Printing House filtered through the workshop walls. Meredith caught fragments of heated debate about Dickens's latest serial. A burst of laughter punctuated someone's critique of the newspaper's political cartoon.

Her nose twitched at a new scent drifting through the window — the sweet, yeasty aroma of Mrs Cooper's fresh bread. The baker must have just pulled another batch from the brick oven, and the smell mingled with the workshop's leather and glue to create something uniquely comforting. Her stomach growled, reminding her of the meat pies Mrs Cooper often set aside for them.

"That's the third time today," Thomas said, nodding toward the printing house next door. "They're still arguing about that piece on the corn laws."

A sharp rap of knuckles on wood punctuated his words as someone next door pounded a table to emphasise their point. The sound of shuffling papers and the distinctive clank of type being set provided a steady rhythm to the afternoon's work.

"Mrs Cooper's cinnamon buns must be ready," Elizabeth said, marking her place in the book. "I can smell them from here."

The bakery's bell chimed, and voices drifted up from the street — customers gathering for their afternoon treats. Meredith recognised Mr Harrison from the printing house, his distinctive laugh mixing with Mrs Cooper's warm greeting. The sounds of commerce and conversation, of lives intertwining on their small stretch of Paternoster Row, created a melody as familiar as her mother's readings.

She inhaled deeply, savouring the mix of scents — fresh ink and paper from one side, warm bread from the other, and her father's leather and glue at the centre of it all. Each smell told its own story, weaving together into the fabric of their daily life.

The workshop seemed to breathe with life even as day faded. She inhaled deeply. These smells belonged to her father's world, just as her mother's clear alto belonged to the realm of stories. Both crafts, so different yet perfectly matched, lived together in this space.

She pictured herself at her own workbench someday, surrounded by rolls of leather and stacks of paper waiting to be transformed. In her mind's eye, she saw sunshine streaming through windows much like these, illuminating a place where books came alive both inside and out. Her hands would craft beautiful bindings while her voice, like her mother's, would give wings to the words within.

The leather scraps of her journal caught the lamplight, each piece telling its own tale through texture and shade. This patchwork binding represented everything she dreamed of — taking fragments of both her parent's gifts and piecing them together into something uniquely her own. A place where stories could live and breathe, wrapped in covers worthy of their words.

3
ENCROACHING COUGH

SPRING, 1944

The spring rain drummed against the workshop windows, its steady rhythm broken only by Elizabeth's occasional cough. Meredith's hands stilled over her work as her mother's voice caught on the Psalm she was reading. The familiar cadence of Elizabeth's reading faltered, replaced by a dry, rasping sound.

"Just the damp getting into my chest." Elizabeth pressed a handkerchief to her lips. "Where were we? Ah yes — 'that I may dwell in the house of the Lord all the days of my life'."

Meredith watched her mother's fingers tremble slightly as they turned the page. The usual grace of her movements seemed off-kilter, like a book with its spine slightly askew. Elizabeth's eyes, normally bright with the joy of reading, clouded over briefly before she found her place again.

The cough had started three weeks ago. At first, it came only in the mornings, when the fog from the Thames crept through London's streets. But now it interrupted their daily readings more frequently, causing Elizabeth to pause mid-sentence, her voice growing hoarse.

Sunlight broke through the clouds, casting a pale beam across her mother's face. Meredith noticed the slight flush in Elizabeth's cheeks, so different from her usual complexion. When their eyes met, her mother's smile didn't quite reach her eyes as it used to. The sparkle that had illuminated countless stories now seemed dimmed, like a candle struggling against a draft.

"Perhaps we should take a break," Meredith suggested, setting aside the leather she'd been tooling.

"Nonsense." Elizabeth straightened in her chair, squaring her shoulders.

But her next words dissolved into another fit of coughing. This time, the handkerchief stayed pressed to her mouth longer, and when she lowered it, she folded it quickly into her lap.

MEREDITH PICKED at the edge of her workbench, running her nails along the familiar grooves worn smooth by years of craft. Outside, sparrows nested in the eaves, their cheerful songs a stark contrast to the wet, heavy sound of her mother's breathing.

The workshop's usual scents now mingled with the sharp tang of cod liver oil prescribed by Dr Bennett. Her mother's armchair sat empty more often, the indentation in its cushion the only trace of her presence during her increasingly frequent rest periods upstairs.

The doctor's footsteps on their narrow staircase had become as regular as the church bells of St Paul's. His black medical bag knocked against the banister with each visit —

twice last week, three times this week. Each time, Meredith's stomach knotted at the sound.

"Just a touch of bronchitis," he'd said the first time, his voice carrying the same gentle tone he used when setting a child's broken arm or treating a fever.

But his expression changed with each visit. The corners of his mouth pulled tighter, his brow furrowed deeper. He spent longer periods upstairs with Elizabeth, their hushed voices drifting down through the floorboards.

Between visits, Meredith caught glimpses of handkerchiefs disappearing into her mother's pockets, each one bearing telltale spots she pretended not to see. The sound of coughing echoed through their home at all hours now, drowning out even the clatter of Cedar's printing press next door.

Spring bloomed outside their window — purple crocuses pushing through the cracks in the cobblestones, the sweet scent of Mrs Cooper's hot cross buns wafting from next door. But inside, Elizabeth's voice grew weaker, her readings shorter. The familiar passages of Shakespeare and Wordsworth that once filled their days now came in fragments, broken by fits of coughing that left her gasping for air.

The workshop's familiar rhythms changed. Where Elizabeth's voice once painted stories in the air between leather-bound volumes, silence crept in like evening shadows. Thomas hunched over his work table, his fingers moving mechanically. The bone folder slipped from his grip twice that morning — something Meredith had never seen before.

She took over brewing the morning tea, carrying the tray up the narrow stairs to her mother's bedroom. The floorboards creaked beneath her feet as she balanced the cup and saucer, careful not to spill a drop. Elizabeth's smile remained bright, though her face had grown pale as parchment.

Between tasks at her workbench, Meredith swept the

floors, dusted the shelves, and kept the fire stoked. The workshop's brass finishing wheels, usually gleaming from regular polish, had dulled. She cleaned them each evening, trying to maintain some semblance of their former routine.

In the washing basket, beneath layers of cotton and wool, she discovered the growing collection of handkerchiefs. White squares stained with spots of red, carefully folded and hidden away. Her fingers brushed against one, and she pulled back as if burned. Each new addition to the pile marked another day of decline, another piece of evidence her mother tried to conceal.

At night, by candlelight, Meredith wrote in her leather-bound journal. She recorded the small moments — how her mother's hand still stroked her hair during evening prayers, the way she hummed hymns between coughing fits, her quiet delight when Meredith read aloud from 'Pride and Prejudice'. The pages captured fragments of warmth like pressed flowers, preserving them against the growing cold that settled over their home.

The leather cover of her journal bore her mother's favourite quote, tooled in gold: "Books are the windows to the soul." Meredith traced the letters with her finger, remembering how her mother had taught her to appreciate not just the binding of books, but the life within their pages.

4
THE SILENCE

AUTUMN, 1944

Autumn crept through London like a thief, stealing warmth and light. The workshop's walls sweated with dampness, and Elizabeth's chair stood empty, a hollow reminder of evenings past. Meredith's fingers worked the leather of a simple binding, but the rhythmic movements felt wrong without her mother's voice painting stories in the air.

The silence pressed against her ears. No Shakespeare. No Wordsworth. No Bible verses carried on Elizabeth's clear alto. Even the creaking floorboards above seemed to mock the absence of her mother's footsteps.

Thomas cleared his throat. "See how the grain catches the light here?" He held up a piece of calfskin, attempting to spark their usual technical discussions. "Perfect for the spine work on that theological commission."

Meredith nodded, but the words fell flat between them. Her father's attempts at conversation, though well-meaning, only highlighted what was missing. The familiar discussions of craft and technique felt hollow without Elizabeth's literary insights weaving through them.

"Remember how Mother says that each book deserves a binding that matches its soul?" Meredith's voice caught on the words.

Thomas's hands stilled over his work. The bone folder trembled slightly in his grip before he set it down. "She did, didn't she?" He picked up a fresh piece of leather, turning it over and over. "Always knew.. knows exactly which colour would suit each story."

The workshop's familiar scents mingled with the sharp medicines from upstairs. Even Mrs Cooper's fresh-baked bread next door couldn't mask it. Meredith's fingers traced the worn edge of her workbench, remembering how Elizabeth would tap out the rhythm of sonnets against the wood while they worked.

Thomas started another conversation about proper stitch spacing, his voice straining to fill the void. But the words hung in the air like dust motes, unable to replace the warmth of Elizabeth's readings. The silence between his sentences grew longer, heavier, until only the sound of their tools moving across leather remained.

5
ECHOES OF WORDS

Autumn sunlight sliced through Meredith's window, but something felt wrong. The usual morning bustle — her father's footsteps, the kettle's whistle, her mother's quiet humming — all absent. The silence pressed against her as she slipped from beneath her blankets.

The floorboards creaked under her feet as she crossed the landing. No scent of fresh tea wafted up from below, no gentle cough echoed through the walls. Her heart hammered against her ribs as she approached her parents' door.

A sob broke the morning stillness. Meredith pushed the door open to find her father hunched over the bed, his shoulders shaking. Elizabeth lay still beneath the blankets, her face peaceful but devoid of colour. The morning light caught the silver locket at her throat.

Thomas gripped Elizabeth's hand with desperate intensity, pressing it to his weathered cheek as if trying to absorb any lingering warmth. His tears fell steadily onto the bedsheet, darkening the fabric in small circles that spread like ink stains across parchment. Meredith's legs carried her forward without thought, her body moving of its own accord as the familiar smell of her mother's lavender soap filled her nose. She collapsed beside him, her knees striking the hardwood floor with a dull thud that she barely registered through her shock.

They sat together as the sun climbed higher, casting shadows across Elizabeth's face. The stillness felt absolute, broken only by their ragged breathing and the distant sounds of London awakening outside their windows.

Below, the workshop stood silent. No poetry drifted up the stairs, no Shakespeare sonnets or Scripture verses filled the air. The space that once vibrated with Elizabeth's voice now held only echoes, each corner seeming to shrink without her presence to fill it.

Elizabeth's chair by the window sat empty, her latest book still open to the last page she'd read.

Finally, after what felt like years but must have only been a few minutes, Meredith stood and moved gently towards her mother's body. Her fingers found her mother's locket, cool against her palm, as tears blurred her vision. She lifted it with careful fingers, its weight familiar yet strange without Elizabeth's warmth.

The clasp resisted at first. When it finally yielded, Meredith caught her breath. There, preserved in miniature, her parents stood together on their wedding day. Elizabeth's face glowed with joy, her hand tucked into Thomas's arm. The artist had captured her mother's gentle smile, the same one that had brightened their workshop during countless readings.

Meredith's voice cracked. She traced the outline of her mother's face through the glass. "Remember how you told me about this day? The flowers in your hair, the book of sonnets Father gave you..."

The locket's silver surface bore tiny scratches from years of wear, each mark telling its own story. Elizabeth had clutched it during difficult days, during moments of joy, during quiet evenings of reading Shakespeare. Now it lay cold in Meredith's palm, waiting to carry those memories forward.

She pressed the locket to her chest, feeling its edges dig into her skin through her dress. "I'll keep reading, Mother. Every story you loved, every verse that made your eyes light up." Tears splashed onto the silver surface, and she wiped them away with her sleeve. "The workshop won't be silent anymore. I promise."

The words of Romeo and Juliet, of Beatrice and Benedick, of David's Psalms — they all echoed in her mind. Each story lived in the pages they'd bound together, in the leather they'd tooled with careful hands, in the quiet moments between verses when Elizabeth's smile had said more than words ever could.

"Keep it. She'd want you to have it." Her father's voice cracked, but he straightened his back and wiped his face with his sleeve. "Your mother treasured this more than anything except you."

Meredith's throat tightened as she watched her father push himself to his feet. His shoulders hunched forward, as if carrying an invisible weight, but his jaw set with determination.

"I need to..." He paused, drawing a sharp breath. "The undertaker must be called. And arrangements..." His words trailed off as he glanced at Elizabeth's still form.

"I'll help." Meredith slipped the locket around her neck, its weight settling against her collar bone. "I can clean the house, prepare meals—"

"No." Thomas shook his head, then softened his tone. "No, you shouldn't have to worry about such things." He smoothed his waistcoat with shaking hands. "I must speak with Reverend Mills about the funeral arrangements. Your mother always admired the flowers in St Michael's churchyard."

Meredith stood beside him, her hand finding his. "Then I'll make sure the workshop stays organised while you're gone. Mother wouldn't want the orders delayed."

Thomas's fingers tightened around hers. A ghost of pride flickered across his face, breaking through the grief for just a moment. "You're so much like her. The same strength, the same dedication."

The locket pressed against Meredith's skin as she embraced her father. "We'll manage together," she whispered. "Just as Mother would want."

6
BURNT GLUE

Meredith descended the creaking stairs into the workshop, each step weighted with the unfamiliar scent of burnt hide glue that shouldn't have been left on the heat. Her father hunched over his workbench, his shirt wrinkled from sleep that couldn't have lasted more than an hour or two.

Scattered papers surrounded him, covered in his usually precise handwriting now turned jagged and rushed. Numbers and dates filled the margins — calculations for the multitude of commissions that seemed to consume his every waking moment.

The workshop felt different in the dim light of dawn. Shadows crept between the brass finishing wheels that hung in neat rows, tools her father had collected over decades of work. A thin layer of dust coated the shelves of leather samples – everything from simple calfskin to the exotic snake leather they saved for special commissions.

Her mother's chair stood empty by the window, the first rays of sunlight catching the worn fabric where Elizabeth had spent countless hours reading. The silence pressed against Meredith's ears. No poetry. No Shakespeare. No Bible verses floating through the air as her father worked.

Thomas's hands trembled as he reached for another piece of leather, his fingers cracked and bleeding from too many hours spent in water and chemicals. Dark circles shadowed his eyes, deeper than Meredith had ever seen them. He'd barely looked up when she entered, lost in his desperate race against time and grief.

The hide glue pot still simmered on its stand, forgotten in the night. The burnt smell grew stronger as Meredith moved to remove it from the heat. Her father had always been so careful with his tools, but now papers lay scattered across the floor, leather scraps fell where they might, and the usually pristine workbench bore stains from spilled adhesive.

Meredith watched her father reach for another sheet of paper, his hand shaking as he recorded yet another commission in his ledger. The names and dates blurred together — three Bibles for the Whitworth family, a collection of poetry for Lady Ashton, and now another Dickens for Mr Greensworth. Each entry represented hours of meticulous work that would stretch deep into the night.

Her father's fingers left smudges of blood on the white paper. The constant exposure to water and chemicals had cracked his skin raw, but he wouldn't stop. Couldn't stop. The workshop that had once been filled with the gentle rhythm of pages being sewn now thundered with desperate energy.

Thomas rose from his bench, swaying slightly from exhaustion. His eyes fixed on the highest shelf where he kept the finest materials. With trembling hands, he pulled down a roll of creamy calfskin leather. The material unfurled with a soft whisper that reminded Meredith of turning pages.

Her father's fingers traced the grain of the leather,

following its natural patterns. For a moment, his face softened. This was the kind of leather her mother had loved best — smooth as silk but strong enough to protect centuries of words. Elizabeth used to say you could feel the story in the texture of the binding, that each piece of leather had its own tale to tell.

"Perfect for the... Hmm..." Thomas muttered, measuring the hide against his forearm. "Need to... Can't disappoint..." His voice cracked on the last word, but his hands remained steady on the leather, clinging to this one familiar comfort in a world that had tilted off its axis.

He had been like this ever since Elizabeth's death. Almost two months now.

Meredith watched her father smooth the leather with practiced strokes, his movements growing more focused with each pass of the bone folder. The familiar rhythm seemed to steady him, though his shoulders remained tense beneath his worn shirt.

"Father, shall I prepare the end papers for the Whitworth commission?" Her voice sounded small in the workshop's heavy silence.

Thomas didn't look up from his work. His cracked fingers continued their methodical path across the leather. "No need. I'll handle it."

The words came out clipped, distracted. He reached for one of his many tools, testing the edge against his thumb before returning to the task. The leather yielded beneath his touch as he worked it into the spine's curves.

Meredith picked up a fallen scrap of Morocco leather, running her fingers along its grain. "Mother always said this burgundy shade reminded her of—"

"The end papers are in the top drawer." Thomas cut her off, his voice rough. "Best get started on those signatures for the Greensworth commission instead."

She set down the leather and moved toward the workbench, careful not to disturb the scattered papers. Her father had retreated into his own world again, one bound by leather and thread where grief couldn't touch him. His hands never stopped moving — measuring, cutting, folding — as if stillness might shatter the fragile peace he found in his craft.

The workshop felt smaller these days, compressed by the weight of words left unsaid. Thomas worked longer hours, taking on more commissions than ever before. When Meredith brought him tea or bread from Mrs Cooper's, he'd barely pause long enough to take a sip or bite before returning to his endless tasks.

She gathered the loose signatures, aligning their edges with care. Her father's soft muttering filled the silence — calculations and measurements tumbling together as he lost himself in the familiar motions of his trade.

7
MRS COOPER

Jane Cooper wiped flour from her hands onto her well-worn apron and breathed in the familiar scent of fresh bread. Through the bakery's front window, dawn painted Paternoster Row in shades of amber. Her weathered hands pressed into another batch of dough, working it with practiced motions learned over decades at this very counter.

The brass bell above her door chimed as Mr Oak collected his morning loaf. His ink-stained fingers left faint marks on the coins he placed in her palm.

"Smells divine as always, Mrs Cooper." He inhaled deeply, his moustache twitching with appreciation.

Jane's laugh echoed off the worn wooden shelves lined with cooling bread. "Fresh from the oven, just how you like it." She wrapped the steaming loaf in brown paper, her fingers moving with natural grace.

The warmth from her ovens spilled onto the street through the open door, carrying the aroma of baking bread. Early morning workers paused in their hurried steps, drawn by the promise of sustenance and comfort. Jane watched them through the window, her heart swelling with pride at how her little shop brought light to their lives.

She hummed as she worked more dough, her strong arms kneading in smooth, steady motions. The familiar rhythm brought memories of teaching her daughter years ago, before consumption had claimed her. Now she poured that maternal energy into caring for the neighbourhood's children, ensuring none went hungry.

The growing light cast long shadows across her well-scrubbed floor. Steam rose from fresh loaves cooling on racks, dancing in the golden rays that streamed through her front window. Her joy showed in every movement as she prepared for another day of feeding her community.

Jane kneaded her dough with extra vigor, watching Thomas Aldrich through the bakery window. His shoulders slumped as he trudged past Cedar's Printing House, dark circles carved beneath his eyes. The morning light caught his face, revealing skin stretched tight over cheekbones that hadn't been so prominent last month.

Her hands stilled in the dough. Thomas stumbled on a loose cobblestone, catching himself against the wall. The leather satchel at his side bulged with what she recognized as another stack of bookbinding work.

The bell above her door chimed as he entered, the scent of fresh bread mixing with the sharp tang of hide glue that clung to his clothes. His hands trembled as he placed three pennies on her counter.

"Morning, Mr Aldrich." Jane brushed flour from her apron, noting how his waistcoat hung loose where it had once fit trim.

He managed a weak nod, his cracked fingers leaving traces of blood on the brown paper as she wrapped his daily loaf. The veins in his hands stood out stark and blue against pale skin.

"Poor man, he's working himself to the bone," she whispered under her breath as the door closed behind him. Her fingers pressed deeper into the dough, working out her worry through the familiar motions of her craft.

Through the window, she watched him disappear into his workshop, his steps heavy with exhaustion. The dough beneath her hands felt soft and alive, unlike the stiffness that had crept into Thomas's movements.

The morning sun caught the brass numbers on his door — 42 Paternoster Row — where Elizabeth's voice had once carried Shakespeare's sonnets into the street. Now only silence spilled from the workshop, broken by the rhythmic sound of Thomas's bone folder working leather into submission.

Jane pulled another batch of rolls from the oven, her mind drifting to young Meredith. Through her window, Jane caught glimpses of the child darting between market stalls, her once-neat appearance growing more disheveled with each passing day.

Her heart ached watching Meredith manage tasks that should fall to someone twice her age. The girl balanced baskets of supplies, rushing back to their workshop with determination etched across her young face. Dark circles shadowed her eyes, mirroring those of her father.

Jane's hands trembled as she arranged the fresh rolls, remembering how Elizabeth would bring Meredith here for warm treats after their reading sessions. The child's laughter had filled these walls, her eyes bright as she shared tales from whatever story her mother had read that day.

"Such a burden for such small shoulders," Jane murmured, watching Meredith hurry past with an armful of leather supplies. The girl's pinafore hung loose where it had once fit properly, and her hair escaped its ribbon in wild tangles.

The sight reminded Jane of her own daughter's struggles

before the consumption took her. She recognised the look of a child forced to grow up too fast, shouldering responsibilities that should never be theirs to bear. Meredith now carried not only her own grief but also her father's sorrow, trying to hold together what remained of their family.

Through her window, Jane watched Meredith pause to adjust her load, her thin arms straining under the weight of the leather and tools. The silver locket – Elizabeth's locket – caught the morning light as it swung from the girl's neck, a precious reminder of what she'd lost.

JANE KNEADED her last batch of dough with extra vigour, her mind fixed on the gaunt face she'd seen that morning. The empty workshop windows had grown dark, but a single candle still flickered behind the glass. Thomas hadn't stopped working since dawn.

Her weathered hands shaped meat pies with practiced ease, the steam rising as she pulled them from the oven. The rich aroma of beef and gravy filled her small kitchen. She'd added extra meat today, remembering how Thomas's clothes hung loose on his frame.

The street had grown quiet, most shops closed for the night. Only the occasional clip of hooves on cobblestones broke the silence. Jane wrapped three warm loaves and two meat pies in brown paper, her fingers creating neat folds and corners.

She dipped her pen in ink, the nib scratching against small pieces of paper as she wrote five identical notes. Her letters flowed across the page, steady and clear: "For my dear neighbour. Do take care, Thomas! Love, Mrs Cooper."

The notes tucked carefully into each parcel, Jane gathered

them in her arms. The packages radiated warmth against her chest as she approached number 42.

Candlelight still flickered in the workshop window. The steady tap of Thomas's bone folder drifted down to the street.

Jane placed the parcels on his doorstep, arranging them so he couldn't miss them when he finally emerged.

8

A NEW COMMISSION

SPRING, 1846

Meredith sorted through the morning's post, her fingers lingering on a thick envelope. The Carter family crest caught the weak winter light – a lion rampant against crossed quills. She carried it to her father's workbench, where he hunched over a half-finished binding.

"Father, look." She placed the envelope beside his tools.

Thomas's hands trembled as he broke the seal. Candlelight flickered across his gaunt face as his eyes darted across the page. A sharp intake of breath made him cough.

"The Carters want their theological collection bound." His voice cracked. "All twenty volumes."

Meredith's heart leapt. The Carters were known throughout London for their library. Such a commission might allow them to pay off their mounting debts. Her father had done his best to hide them from Meredith, but at fourteen, she was a lot sharper and smarter than she had been at eleven.

Thomas spread the letter flat on his bench, smoothing the

heavy parchment with calloused fingers. "Three months to complete the work. Full morocco binding, gilt edges, hand-tooled spines..."

His voice trailed off as he studied the detailed specifications. Meredith watched his shoulders sag under the commission's demands. Twenty volumes would require careful planning, precise execution, and endless hours of work. Even at his best, with Elizabeth alive and his health intact, such a task would have challenged him.

"We can do this together," Meredith said, reaching for his arm. "I can help with the sewing and forwarding—"

"No." Thomas folded the letter with decisive movements. "This commission must be perfect. The Carters expect nothing less than excellence." He pulled a fresh sheet of paper from his desk drawer and began drafting a response, his hands steady for the first time in weeks.

Meredith watched him dip his pen in ink, noting how his spine straightened and his chin lifted. The Carter commission had awakened something in him — a spark of his old determination mixed with desperate resolve.

Through the workshop's grimy windows, weak sunlight caught the dust motes dancing above twenty leather-bound volumes spread across her father's workbench. Meredith watched as Thomas lifted each book with reverence, his fingers tracing the worn spines and testing loose sections.

"The paper quality is exceptional." He opened the first volume, running his palm across the title page. The scent of aged paper filled the air. "Italian laid paper, with just the right tooth for taking ink."

The familiar scratch of his pen against paper pulled at

Meredith's heart. She hadn't heard that sound in months. Thomas filled page after page with notes, measuring dimensions and sketching decorative patterns.

"These will need matching morocco." He held a volume up to the light. "Deep burgundy, with raised bands." His voice gained strength as he spoke. "Gold tooling here, and here." His finger traced imaginary patterns across the spine.

Meredith edged closer, drawn by the spark in his eyes. He pulled out his leather samples, comparing shades and textures. The careful deliberation in his movements reminded her of earlier days, when he would spend hours selecting the perfect materials for each project.

"The endpapers must be marbled." He sketched quick patterns in his notebook. "Blues and gold to complement the leather." His pen moved faster, capturing ideas that seemed to pour from him. "And look here—" He gestured to a particularly ornate volume. "We'll echo these original tooling patterns, but refined. More elegant."

The workshop felt warmer somehow, filled with the energy of creation rather than the hollow echo of loss. Thomas's hands, though still bearing the marks of recent injuries, moved with their old precision as he documented every detail of the collection before him.

9
WORK

Meredith watched her father from the workshop doorway. His fingers trembled as he pulled thread through signatures, the needle catching light from the guttering candle. The clock struck midnight, but Thomas showed no sign of stopping. Fifteen volumes remained, and the Carter deadline loomed like a storm cloud.

"Father, Mrs Cooper gave us some fresh bread." Meredith placed the still-warm loaf on the corner of his workbench.

Thomas didn't look up. "Set it there."

The bread from yesterday sat untouched, gone stale beside a half-empty cup of cold tea. Her father's face had grown gaunt, skin pulled tight across his cheekbones. Dark circles shadowed his eyes, and his hands bore fresh cuts from the sharp needles and thread.

"The kettle's hot if you'd like—"

"Not now." Thomas reached for another signature, his movements mechanical. "These signatures won't sew themselves."

Meredith lingered by the door, counting the hours since

she'd last seen him eat. The workshop air hung thick with the scent of hide glue and leather, mingling with the mustiness of paper and the sharp tang of brass polish. Her father's shoulders hunched over the sewing frame, his spine curved like the arc of his binding needle.

Dawn's pale light crept through the workshop windows, casting long shadows across the floor. Still Thomas worked, pausing only to flex his cramping fingers before returning to the endless cycle of sewing, gluing, and pressing. The steady tap of his bone folder against leather filled the silence where conversation used to live.

"The pastries are still warm." Meredith set a paper-wrapped bundle beside the untouched bread.

Thomas nodded vaguely, eyes fixed on aligning the spine of volume eight. His fingers shook as he reached for the glue pot, splattering drops across his worn waistcoat.

The workshop clock struck five. Another day began, indistinguishable from the last. Meredith watched her father dip his head back to his work, knowing he'd remain there until exhaustion forced his eyes closed or his body refused to continue.

10
THE COST

Meredith watched her father's hands shake as he reached for his bone folder. The simple movement seemed to drain him, each gesture a battle against his own failing strength. His skin had taken on a sickly pallor, and his clothes hung loose on his frame. Even the act of threading a needle now took several attempts, his fingers trembling too much to find the eye.

The workshop table bore evidence of his decline – bloodstained rags wrapped around his cracked fingers, half-drunk cups of tea gone cold, and bread crusts hardening in forgotten corners. Thomas stared at his tools, his eyes unfocused, while his hands throbbed visibly with each pulse of his heart.

A small photograph slipped from between the volumes – her mother's face smiled up from the worn paper. Thomas's expression softened as he picked it up. His fingers traced the edge of the image, and for a moment, Meredith glimpsed a shadow of joy cross his features. She remembered how her mother would lean over his shoulder, praising the precision of his gold tooling or the elegance of his morocco bindings.

The tenth volume of the Carter commission sat completed before him, its burgundy leather gleaming in the lamplight. Thomas ran his palm across the cover, testing the smoothness of his work. Pride mingled with sadness in his eyes as he examined the crisp corners and even stitching.

His fingertips traced the spine's raised bands, lingering on each ridge as if searching for something beyond the physical craftsmanship. The familiar scent of leather and glue filled the air, but Meredith noticed how her father's touch seemed to seek something more — perhaps the echo of Elizabeth's presence in the perfectly executed work.

Meredith recognised that each volume her father completed wasn't merely about fulfilling the Carter family's expectations. Every stitch, every careful application of leather, every moment spent hunched over his workbench connected him to the life they'd shared with Elizabeth. But the cost of maintaining that connection showed in his trembling hands and hollow cheeks.

Meredith grabbed her leather apron from its hook. "Father, let me help with the forwarding. I can—"

"No." Thomas yanked the half-bound volume closer to his chest. "Your hands aren't ready for morocco."

"But you taught me how to—"

"I said no." His voice cracked. Blood seeped through the cloth wrapped around his fingers, staining the workbench. "Go upstairs. Get some sleep."

"You're the one who needs rest." Meredith reached for his bandaged hand. "Your fingers are bleeding again."

Thomas pulled away, knocking over an empty teacup. "I won't have you breathing in these fumes. The chemicals..." He broke into a coughing fit that bent him double.

"Just like mother—" The words slipped out before Meredith could stop them.

Thomas's head snapped up, his grey eyes wild. "That's exactly why you can't be here. I won't lose you too." He pressed his palm against his chest, struggling to catch his breath. "This commission will secure your future. The Carters pay well."

"But father—"

"Please." Thomas gripped the edge of the workbench, his knuckles white. "Let me do this for you. I couldn't save your mother, but I can ensure you're provided for."

Meredith's throat tightened as she watched him pick up his bone folder with trembling fingers. The lamplight caught the silver threads in his hair — when had they appeared? His shoulders hunched as he smoothed the leather, each movement a battle against exhaustion.

She knew arguing would only drive him to work harder. The determination in his eyes matched the set of his jaw — the same expression he'd worn through her mother's illness, through the endless nights of trying to save her.

11
FOR THE FUTURE

SUMMER, 1846

Thomas's fingers trembled as he smoothed the burgundy morocco leather over the boards of the fifteenth volume. The candle's flame wavered. His bones ached, but he couldn't stop — wouldn't stop. Not with only five volumes remaining after this one.

He reached for the bone folder, the smooth ivory worn from years of use. The tool felt heavier tonight, each stroke requiring more effort than the last. The leather responded under his touch, moulding to the boards just as it had done countless times before.

Sweat trickled down his temple despite the workshop's chill. The familiar scent of hide glue filled his nostrils, mingling with the sharp tang of the finishing oil. His cracked hands left faint traces of blood on the leather, which he quickly wiped away with his cloth.

The stack of completed volumes loomed beside him, fourteen

perfect bindings that would secure Meredith's future. He glanced at Elizabeth's empty chair by the window, remembering how she used to read while he worked. The silence pressed against his ears.

Thomas dipped his brush in the glue pot, the thickness telling him it needed heating again. But he couldn't spare the time. Each moment spent away from the binding was a moment wasted. His vision blurred as he applied the adhesive, forcing him to lean closer to the workbench.

The flame guttered in a draft, sending shadows dancing across the walls. Stacks of paper waited like ghosts in the corners, patient for their turn under his hands. He fumbled with the finishing tools, their brass surfaces catching what little light remained.

His fingers moved automatically through the familiar motions – fold, press, smooth, repeat. The leather gradually took shape under his ministrations, though the work seemed to move slower than usual. Still, he pressed on. The Carters would have their books, perfect in every detail, even if it took his last breath to complete them.

Thomas's hands shook as he pulled another length of thread through the signatures. "Three days," he muttered, his voice hoarse from disuse. "Three days until the deadline." The needle slipped in his grip, and he took in a sharp breath, forcing his trembling fingers to steady.

The leather beneath his hands blurred, then sharpened. He blinked hard, trying to focus on the precise stitches required for the Carter commission. Each movement felt like lifting lead weights, but he couldn't stop. Not now. Not when Meredith's future hung in the balance.

"She has your talent, Elizabeth," he whispered to the empty chair. "But she needs security. A proper future." His shoulders ached as he hunched closer to the work, squinting in the dim light. The bone folder slipped from his grasp, clattering against the workbench.

The rhythmic pierce and pull of the needle through leather became hypnotic. In, out. In, out. Like a lullaby his mother used to sing. The workshop seemed to sway around him, tools and leather dancing at the edges of his vision. His head felt impossibly heavy, yet light as air.

Thomas gripped the workbench with one hand, the partially finished volume clutched in the other. The room tilted sharply. He tried to straighten, to shake off the fog clouding his mind, but his body refused to obey. The candlelight stretched and twisted before his eyes.

His last conscious thought was of the unfinished binding as darkness swept over him. The book remained trapped in his rigid fingers as his head dropped forward onto the workbench.

12

DAWN

The morning sun slanted through the workshop's grimy window, casting long shadows across the leather-strewn workbench. Dust motes danced in the golden beam, undisturbed by the usual sounds of Thomas's work. No creak of the finishing press, no scratch of tools against leather, no muttered calculations of measurements.

Meredith's bare feet found each familiar creaky step as she descended from their living quarters. Her nightdress caught on a loose nail, and she tugged it free, the small tear joining others she'd meant to mend. The scent of fresh bread wafted from next door, accompanied by the clatter of Mrs Cooper's pans and the murmur of early customers.

The workshop door stood ajar. Strange — Father always closed it at night to keep the leather protected from dampness. The brass bell above remained silent, though a draft stirred the pages of open ledgers scattered across the cutting table.

"Father?" Her voice cracked from sleep.

The silence pressed against her, broken only by the distant rumble of cart wheels on cobblestones and a cat yowling in the alley. Even Cedar's printing press next door remained quiet, too early for the day's work to begin.

A strip of sunlight illuminated Thomas's workbench, where the fifteenth volume of the Carter commission lay unfinished, its half-attached spine gaping like an open wound. Thomas's favourite finishing tools lay scattered, their brass surfaces dulled with dried paste.

Meredith's heart slammed in her chest as she caught sight of her father. He was slumped over the edge of the workbench, his head resting against the leather-covered boards of the Carter volume. Her feet carried her across the workshop floor before her mind could process the scene.

"Father?" The word caught in her throat.

Thomas didn't stir. His skin held the colour of old parchment, a sickly pallor that made her stomach twist. She pressed her fingers to his neck, the way Dr Bennett had shown her when checking Elizabeth's pulse. His skin felt cool beneath her touch.

Her gaze fell to his hands. They curled around the bone folder — the same tool his father had used to shape countless spines and smooth endless sheets of paper. The ivory surface bore the marks of three generations of bookbinders, its patina deepened by years of use. Thomas's fingers wrapped around it as if protecting this piece of their heritage even in unconsciousness.

The bone folder had been the first tool Thomas had ever placed in her hands. "This belonged to your grandfather," he'd told her. "One day it will be yours." Now those words echoed in her mind as she stared at his grip on their family's legacy.

Memories crashed over Meredith like waves. Her mother's voice floated through her mind, clear as yesterday, reading from Romeo and Juliet while Thomas worked the leather with practiced hands. The remembered laughter pierced her heart

— her mother's gentle chuckle, and her father's deep rumble when Meredith would mix up her tools.

Her fingers traced the worn edge of the workbench where she'd spent countless hours watching Thomas shape leather into art. The ghost of his hands guiding hers over smooth calfskin, teaching her the grain's secrets. "Feel that?" he'd say. "The leather speaks to us."

The morning sun caught dust motes swirling above Thomas's still form, dancing like the sparks that used to fly from the finishing iron when he worked late into the night. She remembered the pride in his eyes when she'd sewn her first signature, the way he'd displayed her crooked stitches as if they were masterworks.

Her throat closed as she recalled their last proper meal together, bread from Mrs Cooper's still warm on the table. Thomas had barely touched it, too focused on the Carter commission. The bread had gone stale, untouched like Elizabeth's empty chair.

Meredith's hands shook as she clutched her mother's silver locket. Inside, Elizabeth smiled from her wedding portrait, forever young and healthy. The metal warmed against her palm as memories of morning readings flooded back — Shakespeare, Wordsworth, the Psalms that had comforted them all.

A sharp knock at the workshop door shattered the stillness. Meredith's fingers tightened around the locket as Mrs Cooper's familiar voice called through the gap.

"Good morning, loves. Brought you some fresh pastries, still warm from the—"

The door creaked wider. Cloth-wrapped bundles tumbled from Mrs Cooper's arms, hitting the floor with dull thuds. The smell of butter and sugar filled the workshop, a cruel contrast to the scene before them.

"Oh, my dear girl." Mrs Cooper's skirts rustled as she

rushed forward, wrapping her arms around Meredith. The baker's hands were warm and flour-dusted, so different from Thomas's cold fingers still curved around the bone folder. "Let me see to this now. You're not alone."

Meredith pressed her face into Mrs Cooper's shoulder, breathing in the comforting scent of yeast and fresh bread that always clung to her apron. The fabric grew damp beneath her cheeks, and she realised she was crying.

"I found him like this." Meredith's voice came out small and broken. "He wouldn't stop working on the Carter books. I tried to make him rest, but—"

"Hush now." Mrs Cooper's hand smoothed Meredith's tangled hair, the gesture so like Elizabeth's that it made Meredith's chest ache. "You did everything you could, love. Let me help."

13
OUT OF HOUSE AND HOME

Mr Roland Sands' towering frame seemed to overshadow Meredith entirely.

"Miss Aldrich." His mouth twisted into a thin line as he adjusted his cravat. Around them, the empty workshop gaped like an open wound.

The past week had blurred together in her mind. Mrs Cooper's steady presence had guided her through the darkness, arranging for the undertakers to carry Thomas away. The baker's flour-dusted hands had helped dress him in his best suit.

The funeral at St Michael's had been small — just her, Mrs Cooper, and a handful of customers who'd known Thomas's craft. No family remained to mourn him. The church's stone walls had amplified the hollow echo of the priest's words as they lowered Thomas into the ground beside Elizabeth.

Now the workshop stood stripped bare. Sunlight filtered through grimy windows where her mother's armchair once caught the morning rays. The workbench where she'd learned to sew signatures sat cold and empty, its surface scarred from years of use. Even the familiar scent of leather and glue had faded, replaced by dust and absence.

"Three months behind on rent." Mr Sands' voice cut through her memories. He pulled a ledger from his coat pocket, thick fingers tracing the columns of figures. "Your father's death, while unfortunate, doesn't erase the debt. You'll need to vacate the premises. Immediately."

The words struck harder than any finishing hammer. This place held every memory she had – her mother reading Shakespeare by candlelight, her father teaching her to work the leather with gentle hands, the laughter that once filled these rooms like music.

Meredith's fingers trembled against the oilcloth bundle. The emptiness of the workshop pressed against her chest, making it hard to breathe. Everything familiar had been stripped away – the leather samples that once lined the walls in neat rows, the brass finishing wheels that caught the morning light, even the stack of marbled papers her father had ordered from Italy last spring.

She'd known this day approached. Mr Sands' men had appeared like shadows over the past week, carrying away pieces of her life one by one. The workbench where she'd pricked her fingers learning to sew signatures. The shelves that had held a hundred stories bound in leather and dreams. Her mother's armchair, where Elizabeth's voice had brought words to life.

Her father's words echoed in her mind: "A true craftsman never gives up." But doubt crept through her veins like ice water. What use were his lessons now, in a world that had taken everything?

Her hand brushed against the silver locket at her throat, and tears threatened to spill. She blinked them back fiercely.

Crying wouldn't change anything. Instead, she knelt beside the remaining bundle of her father's tools.

The bone folder felt smooth against her palm as she wrapped it carefully in the oilcloth. Three needles, worn but sharp, each one representing hours of patient instruction. Her awl which she learn how to skillfully use. His finest finishing wheels, their patterns etched not just in brass but in her memory.

"I'll make you proud, Father," she whispered, securing the bundle with twine. Each knot felt like a promise — to preserve his craft, to honour his memory, to survive despite the crushing weight of loss that threatened to overwhelm her.

Meredith clutched the oilcloth bundle against her chest as she rose from the floor.

"Please, Mr Sands." The words caught in her throat. "Just a few more days to—"

"A few more days?" His light blue eyes narrowed, cold as frost on a window pane. "And what good would that do? The rent remains unpaid." He tapped his ledger with a thick finger, the leather cover creaking. "Your father's death changes nothing. Business is business."

The emptiness of the workshop pressed in around her. Dust motes danced in the shaft of sunlight where her mother's armchair once stood. The bare walls seemed to mock her desperate plea.

"I could work." Meredith's voice shook. "Help in the building, clean the—"

"A child?" Mr Sands's lip curled. "What use would you be? No, Miss Aldrich, I've lost enough income on your family's account." He adjusted his cravat, the silk gleaming against his neck. "The premises must be cleared today. I have new tenants arriving tomorrow morning."

The finality in his tone crushed what little hope remained.

Meredith saw no trace of sympathy in his face, only the stern calculation of profits and losses. To him, she was merely a line item in his ledger, a poor investment to be written off.

Her shoulders slumped under the weight of his words. The bundle in her arms held all that remained of her father's craft, of her family's legacy. Everything else had been stripped away, carried off piece by piece like dead leaves in a cruel wind.

Meredith stumbled onto Paternoster Row. The familiar street had transformed into something unfamiliar and hostile. Horse hooves clattered against cobblestones, the sound hammering through her skull. A fishmonger's cry pierced the air, making her flinch. The press of bodies felt suffocating after the hollow quiet of the workshop.

She pressed herself against the wall, trying to make herself smaller as a cart laden with printing supplies rumbled past. The wheel splashed through a puddle, spattering her skirts with mud. No one noticed. No one cared. Faces blurred past — merchants haggling over goods, ladies in fine dresses consulting shopping lists, children chasing hoops between market stalls.

The world spun around her in a dizzying whirl of colour and noise. Her legs trembled, threatening to give way. Her bag seemed to grow heavier with each passing moment, as if weighted down by all she had lost. The locket at her throat felt like it was choking her.

This street had been her whole world once. She knew every crack in the pavement, every shadowed doorway, every shortcut between buildings. Now it felt vast and threatening, full of dark corners where danger might lurk. She was adrift in an ocean of strangers, without anchor or compass to guide her.

The scent of fresh bread wafted from Mrs Cooper's bakery next door. Through the window, Meredith caught a glimpse of the baker's kind face as she served customers, her movements quick and practiced. The sight of something so normal, so unchanged, made Meredith's chest ache. Mrs Cooper had been there through everything – bringing food when Thomas worked late, offering comfort when Elizabeth passed, helping prepare Thomas for burial. She alone remained constant while Meredith's world crumbled.

14
THE BAKER'S KINDNESS

The bell above Mrs Cooper's door chimed as Meredith stepped inside. The scent of fresh bread and warm pastries wrapped around her like a blanket, familiar and comforting after the harsh reality of the street. Steam rose from fresh loaves cooling on wooden racks, and the heat from the ovens caressed cold cheeks.

The bakery's worn floorboards creaked beneath her feet, each board telling its own story through years of faithful service. Copper pans hung in neat rows along the walls, their surfaces reflecting the morning light that streamed through the front window. The display counter gleamed, lined with meat pies and sweet treats under glass domes.

"Meredith, love." Mrs Cooper emerged from behind the counter, flour dusting her apron and wisps of dark hair escaping her practical bun. Her bright brown eyes crinkled with concern as she took in Meredith's trembling form.

Before Meredith could speak, Mrs Cooper's arms enveloped her in a warm embrace that smelled of yeast and cinnamon.

The baker's solid presence steadied her, and Meredith's fingers clutched at the rough fabric of Mrs Cooper's apron. The bundle of tools pressed between them, a physical reminder of all she'd lost.

"There now, child," Mrs Cooper's voice vibrated through her chest where Meredith's head rested. The simple kindness in those words threatened to unlock the tears Meredith had been holding back since Mr Sands had delivered his verdict.

Mrs Cooper led Meredith up the narrow staircase in the back of the bakery. Each step groaned under their feet, worn smooth from years of use. The warmth from the bakery's ovens below seeped through the floorboards, fighting back the chill that had settled in Meredith's b

ones.

The baker's home opened before them — a simple room with a sturdy table. A fire crackled in the hearth, casting dancing shadows across the whitewashed walls. The flames reminded Meredith of evenings in the workshop, when her father would work by candlelight and her mother's voice would fill the air with Shakespeare's words.

Mrs Cooper pulled out a chair. "Sit, child."

Meredith sank into the offered seat, her bundle of tools clutched tight in her lap. The wooden bowl before her gleamed, well-worn but clean, beside a pewter spoon that caught the firelight. Steam rose from a black pot hanging over the fire, carrying the rich scent of beef and vegetables through the room.

Mrs Cooper's skirts rustled as she moved to the hearth. She lifted the pot with practiced ease, her movements steady as she ladled thick stew into their bowls. The rich brown broth swirled with carrots and potatoes, chunks of meat nestled between them.

A small smile tugged at Meredith's lips as Mrs Cooper settled into her own chair, but Meredith's fingers wouldn't release their grip on the oilcloth bundle. Her throat tightened around unspoken words. The fire popped and hissed, filling the silence between them.

The stew's aroma brought back memories of her mother's cooking, of family meals shared around their own table. Her chest ached with the weight of it all — the workshop stripped bare, her father's workbench empty, Mr Sands' cold eyes as he'd ordered her out. She stared into her bowl, watching the steam rise in delicate curls, while her mind raced with questions about tomorrow, and the day after, and all the days to come.

Mrs Cooper's spoon clinked against her bowl as she stirred her stew. "My Sarah loved to read, just like you." Her eyes fixed on a point beyond the fire. "She'd sit right there by the hearth, nose buried in whatever book she'd borrowed that week."

Meredith's grip on the oilcloth bundle loosened slightly as Mrs Cooper's words painted pictures of another life. The baker's hands, roughened by years of kneading dough, traced patterns on the wooden table.

"Smart as anything, she was. Taught herself French from an old grammar book she found. Used to practice with the customers, especially that professor who came in for his daily loaf." Mrs Cooper's smile carried echoes of pride and pain. "She'd have been twenty-three this spring."

The fire crackled, sending sparks up the chimney. Meredith's chest tightened as she watched Mrs Cooper's fingers brush away a tear. This woman who'd left warm bread on their doorstep, who'd comforted her after finding Father, had carried her own grief in silence all these years.

"She caught the fever during that awful winter of '39." Mrs Cooper's voice dropped to barely more than a whisper. "Three days was all it took. One moment she was translating poetry by the fire, the next..." Her words trailed off into the shadows.

Meredith's throat closed around the bite of stew she'd just taken. The baker's loss echoed her own — an empty chair, a voice silenced too soon. Yet here sat Mrs Cooper, still baking bread, still caring for others despite her own wounds. Such kindness warmed Meredith's heart.

"Sometimes I still hear her laugh when the bell rings." Mrs Cooper's eyes met Meredith's across the table. "Silly, isn't it? But grief does strange things to a mother's heart."

Meredith lifted her spoon. "Thank you, Mrs Cooper." The words came out soft, but the baker's gentle smile showed she'd heard.

The stew filled her stomach with much-needed warmth. Each spoonful brought back strength she hadn't realised she'd lost during the confrontation with Mr Sands. The oilcloth bundle settled in her lap as her grip relaxed, though one hand remained protective over her father's tools.

Mrs Cooper's voice flowed like a gentle stream, sharing memories between bites of stew. "Sarah loved watching the bookbinders work through the window. She'd spend hours sketching their hands as they worked the leather." Her words created a comfortable space around them, asking nothing in return. "She'd have loved your father's finishing work — the way he made each spine unique."

The fire settled in the grate, sending up occasional sparks. Meredith found herself nodding as Mrs Cooper described Sarah's favourite spot in the bakery window, where morning light would catch the dust motes dancing in the air. The baker's memories painted pictures of a girl who'd lived and dreamed in these same rooms, whose presence still lingered in the worn patches on the floorboards and the marks on the windowsill.

"She kept a journal." Mrs Cooper stirred her stew, her spoon catching the firelight. "Filled it with French phrases and poetry. Sometimes I find loose pages tucked between the cookbooks."

The words settled around them like falling leaves, neither heavy nor demanding. Meredith took another spoonful of stew, grateful for the simple comfort of a warm meal and quiet company. Mrs Cooper's stories created a gentle shield against the harsh reality waiting outside, if only for this moment.

The stew settled heavy in Meredith's stomach as Mrs Cooper cleared their bowls.

Mrs Cooper's chair scraped against the floor as she turned to face Meredith. "You are welcome to stay the night, dear." Her voice carried the same gentle tone she'd used when leaving bread on their doorstep, when comforting Meredith after finding Father.

The offer hung in the air between them, thick with unspoken understanding. Meredith's fingers traced the edge of the oilcloth, following the familiar pattern of the binding. Her throat tightened as she looked at Mrs Cooper's kind face, marked by years of both joy and sorrow.

The baker had already lost so much — her Sarah, her dreams of watching her daughter grow. Yet here she sat, offering shelter to another girl who wasn't her own. Such generosity pressed against Meredith's heart, mixing with memories of all the warm loaves and meat pies that had appeared when Father worked through the night.

Meredith's eyes burned as she studied the worn floorboards. Mrs Cooper had already given so much. The thought of adding her own troubles to the baker's burden made her chest ache. She couldn't bear to be another daughter-shaped hole in this kind woman's life, another empty chair by the fire, another name whispered in quiet moments.

The flames cast dancing shadows across Mrs Cooper's face as she waited, patient as rising dough, for Meredith's response. In those shadows, Meredith saw echoes of her own mother's absence, of her father's final night at his workbench. The baker's offered kindness felt like a lifeline thrown into deep waters, yet Meredith's hand hesitated to grasp it.

"Yes, thank you." Meredith's voice caught in her throat. "I would be grateful to stay."

Mrs Cooper's smile warmed the room more than the hearth. She bustled about, gathering blankets and pillows with practiced efficiency. Her movements reminded Meredith of her mother preparing for bedtime, though she pushed the thought away before it could sting.

The baker's room welcomed Meredith with soft lamplight and the lingering scent of fresh bread that seemed to permeate everything Mrs Cooper owned. A makeshift bed appeared on the floor beside the larger one, crafted from quilts and cushions. The centerpiece was a tufted coverlet splashed with deep reds and blues, its surface adorned with delicate flowers stitched in golden thread. Each petal spoke of hours spent with needle and thread, of quiet evenings by candlelight.

Personal touches filled every corner — a small shelf of worn books, a collection of pressed flowers in frames, and a carved wooden box that sat on the bedside table. The room felt lived-in, peaceful in a way that eased the tightness in Meredith's chest.

She settled onto the makeshift bed, the quilt soft beneath her fingers. The oilcloth bundle of tools lay beside her pillow. Sleep refused to come despite her exhaustion. Her mind raced through the events of the day — Mr Sands' cold voice, the empty workshop, Mrs Cooper's kindness. The ceiling above held no answers as she traced the familiar weight of her mother's locket against her throat.

The sound of Mrs Cooper's steady breathing filled the room, but Meredith's thoughts wouldn't quiet. Everything had changed so quickly — first Mother, then Father, and now their home. The workshop that had been her whole world stood empty, its shelves stripped bare of the books and tools that had given it life.

15
NOT ANOTHER BURDEN

Moonlight filtered through Mrs Cooper's thin curtains. Meredith turned on her makeshift bed, the quilt rustling beneath her. Sleep refused to claim her despite the late hour and her bone-deep weariness.

Mrs Cooper's steady breathing filled the quiet room. The baker had given so much already — the countless loaves left at their door, the meat pies that appeared when Father worked through the night, and now this shelter when Meredith needed it most. Each act of kindness felt like another weight added to Meredith's shoulders.

The ceiling above offered no comfort as memories of Sarah Cooper surfaced — fragments of stories Mrs Cooper had shared over their evening meal. A daughter lost too soon, leaving behind empty spaces and half-finished dreams. Now here was Meredith, occupying that hollow place beside the baker's bed, accepting care she hadn't earned.

Meredith's fingers found her mother's locket, cool against her throat. The metal warmed beneath her touch as she thought of Mrs Cooper's gentle hands serving the stew, her soft voice sharing memories of Sarah. The baker had already weathered so much loss, yet still opened her heart and home without hesitation.

The thought of becoming another burden, another daughter-shaped void in Mrs Cooper's life, twisted in Meredith's chest like a knife. She couldn't bear to be one more grief for this kind woman to carry. Better to spare Mrs Cooper the pain of watching another girl slip away, leaving nothing but memories and marked pages in cookbooks.

Dawn's first light began to creep across the room. Meredith lay still, listening to Mrs Cooper's breathing, each inhale a reminder of the generosity she didn't deserve. The baker had lost enough. She didn't need Meredith's troubles added to her own.

Meredith eased herself up from the makeshift bed, each movement calculated to avoid disturbing the floorboards. Her father's tools, still wrapped in oilcloth, waited by her side like old friends.

Mrs Cooper's form rose and fell beneath her quilt, her face peaceful in sleep. The baker's wrinkles smoothed away in the dawn light, years falling from her features. A half-smile curved her lips, perhaps dreaming of Sarah or days long past when her bakery first opened.

Meredith's fingers worked quickly, straightening the borrowed blankets with precise movements learned from years of watching her mother make beds. The pillow still held the indent of her head, and she smoothed it away with gentle pats.

Her few possessions fit easily into her arms — the wrapped tools, her mother's locket secure around her neck, and the clothes she wore.

Pausing at the foot of Mrs Cooper's bed, Meredith watched

the baker sleep. In just one evening, she'd shown more kindness than most had offered in all her life. The shared meal, the stories of Sarah, the offered shelter — each act of generosity strengthened Meredith's resolve. Mrs Cooper deserved better than to watch another girl fade away.

The early morning light streamed stronger now, warming the wooden floor beneath Meredith's feet. She stepped carefully around the creaking boards she'd noted the night before, making her way to Mrs Cooper's small writing desk.

Meredith's fingers trembled as she searched Mrs Cooper's desk, careful not to disturb the neat stacks of receipts and order forms. A small scrap of paper caught her eye — the corner of an old market list, blank on one side. Perfect.

She lifted the pencil from its holder, its worn surface smooth against her palm. The familiar motions of writing brought back memories of her mother's reading sessions, her father's patient teachings about paper grain and proper tool handling.

Dear Mrs Cooper, she wrote, her letters careful and measured despite her shaking hand. The words flowed onto the paper like water finding its path downstream. *Your kindness has meant more than I can say. The warmth of your home, the comfort of your food, and most of all, your understanding heart have given me strength when I needed it most.*

A tear splashed onto the paper, threatening to blur the words. Meredith dabbed it away with her sleeve, determined to leave a proper note rather than a water-stained mess.

Thank you for sharing Sarah's memory with me. Thank you for the stew, the bed, and for showing me that goodness still exists in this world. I will carry your generosity in my heart always.

She signed her name at the bottom. The simple act of writing released something inside her chest — an ache she hadn't realised she'd been carrying since her father's death. Mrs Cooper's kindness had wrapped around her like a warm blanket, offering shelter from the storm of loss and uncertainty.

The baker's gentle snores continued behind her as Meredith placed the note where it would be easily found. Each word felt inadequate to express the depth of her gratitude, yet she hoped Mrs Cooper would understand what lay between the lines — the unspoken appreciation for a moment of peace in the midst of chaos.

Meredith laid the note on Mrs Cooper's bedside table, where the morning light would catch the paper's edge. She crept down the bakery stairs, each step chosen with care to avoid the telltale creaks that might wake the kind baker above.

The shop floor still held yesterday's warmth, traces of cinnamon and fresh bread lingering in the air. Memories of countless mornings spent collecting warm loaves from this very spot threatened to root her feet to the floorboards. But she couldn't stay — wouldn't become another daughter-shaped hole in Mrs Cooper's heart.

The door latch clicked softly beneath her fingers. One last breath of bakery air filled her lungs before she eased the door open, slipping through the narrowest gap possible. The metal handle felt cool against her palm as she guided it shut, refusing to let it slam and disturb Mrs Cooper's peace.

Dawn painted the cobblestones in shades of grey and gold, the morning mist still clinging to corners and alleyways. The street that had seemed so overwhelming yesterday now stretched before her. A few early risers — mostly servants and traders — moved through the awakening city, their footsteps echoing off the buildings.

The morning air bit at her cheeks, sharp and clean

compared to the bakery's warm embrace. She inhaled deeply, letting the crisp chill fill her chest. It carried the mingled scents of the city: horse manure, chimney smoke, and underneath it all, a hint of the Thames. The familiar London smell did little to calm her steadily racing heart.

16

TOMMY WILSON

Meredith clutched her father's tools closer as she wandered deeper into London's maze of streets. Each step carried her further from the warmth of Mrs Cooper's bakery, from the familiar stretch of Paternoster Row where books and fresh bread once marked the rhythm of her days.

The morning crowd thickened around her. Workers rushed past, shoulders hunched against the cold, while cart wheels clattered against cobblestones. A group of women outside a millinery shop turned their heads as she passed, their whispers following her like autumn leaves in the wind.

Her legs ached from walking, but she dared not stop. A shopkeeper sweeping his storefront paused mid-stroke, watching her through narrowed eyes until she hurried past. Outside a butcher's shop, two boys about her age pointed and muttered, their faces twisted with a mixture of curiosity and distrust.

The streets grew narrower, darker. Washing lines stretched between buildings like spider webs, casting strange patterns on the ground. A woman yanked her child closer as Meredith approached, her sharp "Keep walking" cutting through the morning air.

The weight of her situation pressed down on her chest. No home. No family. No destination. The oilcloth bundle of tools seemed to grow heavier with each step, yet she couldn't bear to loosen her grip. These streets held none of the comfort she'd known, only suspicious glances and shuttered doors.

Near a grocer's stall, Meredith paused to catch her breath. The owner's eyes fixed on her immediately, his hands moving to cover his display of apples. "Move along, girl. No loitering here."

She backed away, her throat tight. Even the doorways seemed unwelcoming now, their shadows holding unknown threats. A man sleeping in one stirred as she passed, his bloodshot eyes tracking her movement. The message was clear — vulnerability drew attention, and attention meant danger.

Night crept over London, bringing a bone-deep chill that made Meredith's teeth chatter. She huddled deeper into the doorway of an abandoned shop, wrapping her arms around her father's tools. The stone walls offered little shelter from the wind that whistled through the alley's narrow confines.

A burst of laughter cut through the darkness. Meredith pressed herself further into the shadows, heart racing. More voices joined the first — young, spirited, unafraid. She peered around the doorframe.

Down the alley, a small fire cast dancing shadows on brick walls. A group of children crowded around it, passing something between them. Their faces glowed in the firelight as they talked and jostled each other with familiar ease. One boy stood slightly apart from the rest, gesturing as he told some tale that had his companions hanging on every word.

His tousled hair fell across his forehead, and despite his ragged clothes, he carried himself with unmistakable confidence. The others seemed to naturally orient themselves around him, like moths drawn to flame.

The boy paused mid-story, his head tilting as if sensing her gaze. Dark eyes met hers across the distance. Meredith tried to shrink back into the doorway, but it was too late. He was already moving toward her with a fluid grace that spoke of years navigating these streets.

"Well now, what do we have here?" His voice carried none of the menace she'd heard from others that day. Instead, curiosity coloured his words as he stopped a few feet away. "I'm Tommy Wilson." A grin spread across his face, transforming it from street-hardened to almost boyish. "And you look like you could use a bit of warmth."

Meredith hesitated, but Tommy's warm grin and the promise of fire's heat drew her forward. Her muscles ached from hours of walking, and exhaustion clouded her thoughts.

"First rule of the streets — you've got to know where to eat." Tommy guided her toward the flames where the other children parted to make space. "See that bakery on Bell Street? Old Mr Wright puts his day-olds in the alley after sunset. But you've got to be quick — rats get to them if you're not."

He pulled a crust of bread from his pocket and broke it in half, offering her the larger piece. "The butcher on Crown Court saves bones for soup — his wife's soft-hearted. And there's a greengrocer near the church who'll trade sweeping for bruised apples."

Meredith's fingers closed around the bread, still warm from his pocket. She hadn't had anything to eat since the stew Mrs Cooper had given her the night before.

"Watch this," Tommy said, stepping back into the street. He moved with an easy confidence, shoulders squared but relaxed. "You've got to walk like you belong. Head up, but not too high. Swagger puts folk at ease — makes them think you've got somewhere to be."

He demonstrated, weaving between two merchants with fluid grace. "See how they barely notice? That's what you want. Blend in, become part of the crowd. Streets are safer when you're invisible."

The other children nodded in agreement, and Meredith noticed how they all carried themselves with that same assured posture — neither shrinking nor drawing attention.

"Try it," Tommy encouraged, gesturing to the street. Meredith stood, clutching her father's tools. "No, no — loosen up. You're walking like you're afraid someone's going to grab you. That's what makes them notice."

He adjusted her shoulders, taught her to match the rhythm of the crowd. "There you go. Now you're getting it. Walk like you've got business somewhere important, and most folk will let you pass right by."

∽

Dawn painted the sky in murky shades of grey as Tommy led Meredith through a maze of narrow streets. Her feet dragged with exhaustion, but she forced herself to maintain the confident stride he'd taught her. The oilcloth bundle of tools pressed against her chest like an anchor to her past life.

"These buildings been empty since the fire last summer." Tommy's voice dropped to a whisper as they approached a row of abandoned structures. "Most folk avoid them, thinking they're haunted. Makes them perfect for us."

He guided her past crumbling doorways and debris-filled corners, pointing out which spots to avoid. "See that doorway with the broken glass? Looks sheltered, but the draft cuts right through. And that alcove there? Too visible from the street."

They reached a deep recess between two buildings, hidden behind a jutting wall. "This is the sweet spot. Can't see it from the main road, and the wall blocks the wind."

Meredith sank down in the shadows, her bones aching from the night's wanderings. Tommy pulled several ragged blankets from behind a loose brick.

"Always hide your bedding," he said, passing her a threadbare wool cloth. "Otherwise it'll be gone when you need it most."

He settled beside her, close enough that their shoulders touched. The shared warmth seeped through Meredith's thin clothes, and she found herself leaning slightly into it.

"Wrap it tight around your shoulders," Tommy demonstrated with his own blanket. "Tuck your knees up — makes you smaller, keeps more heat in."

Meredith followed his instructions, cradling her father's tools in the space between her chest and knees. The rough wool scratched against her chin, but she welcomed any barrier against the evening chill.

"Sleep light," Tommy murmured, his voice already heavy with exhaustion. "Wake at any noise. Better to be scared of nothing than caught off guard by something."

∽

MEREDITH SHIFTED against the rough wall. The early morning light cast long shadows across Tommy's face as he began to speak of his life on the streets.

"Been out here since I was eight," he said, picking at a loose thread on his blanket. "Ma got the fever, and that was that."

"My mother had consumption." Meredith's voice caught. "She used to read to us while Father worked. Shakespeare mostly."

Tommy's eyes lit up. "Shakespeare? The fellow who wrote about the ghost king?"

"Hamlet." A smile tugged at her lips. "Mother did all the voices."

"Wish I could've heard that." Tommy grinned. "Best story I know is about the three-legged cat that lives behind the fish market."

Their laughter echoed softly in the alcove, and for a moment, Meredith forgot about the cold stones pressing into her back. She traced the outline of her father's bone folder through the oilcloth.

"Father taught me everything about binding books," she said. "The way leather needs to be worked just so, how to measure the signatures perfectly."

"Like how I learned which shopkeepers turn a blind eye when you're hungry?" Tommy nudged her shoulder. "Different skills, same idea — surviving."

Meredith clutched the tools closer, feeling the solid weight of her father's legacy. The morning air bit at her cheeks, but something warm bloomed in her chest — not quite happiness, but perhaps its cousin: hope.

Tommy pulled his blanket tighter. "Get some rest. I'll wake you if anyone comes."

She nodded, curling around her precious bundle. The tools pressed against her heart like a promise — to her father, to herself, to the craft that had defined their family. Even here, among the shadows and cast-offs of London's streets, she could keep that promise alive.

17
A WAY TO SURVIVE

The sun rose over London's rooftops, casting long shadows across St Michael's Church's weathered stone façade. Meredith breathed in the lingering traces of incense that drifted from beneath the heavy wooden doors alongside the biting morning air that nipped at her nose and cheeks.

The first rays of sunlight filtered through the stained glass windows, painting kaleidoscope patterns on the ground near where she and Tommy huddled in the doorway. A chorus of sparrows started their morning song, their cheerful notes mixing with the deep toll of church bells that echoed across the square.

Meredith shifted beneath the threadbare blanket, her muscles stiff from sleeping on cold stone. Two weeks of this new life had taught her body to wake at the slightest sound, though the church bells provided a gentler awakening than most.

Tommy stretched beside her, his yawn breaking through the morning quiet. "Rise and shine," he nudged her shoulder, though she was already alert. They moved with practiced efficiency, folding the blankets and tucking them into their hiding spot behind a loose stone.

Meredith's hands found the familiar shape of the oilcloth bundle. She unwrapped it just enough to check its contents — her father's bone folder, three needles, her awl, and his finest finishing wheels. Each tool carried the stories of generations, worn smooth by careful hands that had crafted countless bindings. She traced the bone folder's edge with her thumb, remembering how her father's fingers had curved around it that final night.

The tools represented more than just implements of trade — they were her heritage, her father's legacy wrapped in simple cloth. Even here, sleeping rough on London's streets, these precious items connected her to who she was, who she'd been raised to be. She rewrapped them carefully, securing the bundle against her chest before rising to face another day.

The crunch of boots on gravel pulled Meredith's attention to the church steps. Reverend Mills approached, his black coat billowing in the morning breeze. His weathered face creased into a gentle smile that reached his hazel eyes.

"Good morning, children." He set down a woven basket near their feet. Steam rose from the covered pot inside, carrying the rich aroma of vegetable soup. Next to it lay a loaf of crusty bread, still warm from the kitchen. "I thought you might appreciate something to start your day."

Tommy's eyes lit up at the sight of food, but he held back, glancing at the Reverend with careful consideration. "Thank you, sir."

"The church kitchen always has extra." Reverend Mills kept his voice low, casual. "No sense in letting it go to waste."

Meredith clutched her bundle of tools closer, but her stomach betrayed her with a loud growl. The Reverend's kind expression reminded her of her father's — that same mix of authority and gentleness.

"I see you most mornings," he said, hands clasped behind his back. "This doorway... well, it provides better shelter than most." He cleared his throat. "I won't interfere with your choices, but know that my door is always open should you need it."

Tommy nodded, already breaking off a piece of bread. "We manage all right, sir."

"Indeed you do." Reverend Mills stepped back, giving them space. "I'll keep an eye out, though. These streets can be unkind after dark." His gaze lingered on Meredith's bundle, but he asked no questions. "God bless you both."

Meredith eyed the scattered papers dotting the church grounds, her fingers itching with familiar purpose. Near the church steps, discarded bulletins fluttered in the morning breeze. The rubbish bin overflowed with expired pamphlets, their edges curling from yesterday's rain.

She crossed the courtyard, gathering sheets one by one. Her mother's voice echoed in her mind: "Every piece of paper has potential, my dear." The morning sun warmed her back as she sorted through her findings, setting aside the cleanest pieces.

Behind a stone bench, more papers caught her eye — announcements from last week's service, their printed words still crisp and legible. She smoothed each one carefully, remembering how her father would press his palm flat against fresh pages, testing their weight and texture.

From her pocket, she pulled out threads salvaged from seamstresses' bins — blues and browns tangled together. Her fingers worked the knots free, muscle memory taking over as she tested each strand's strength. The thread stretched between her thumbs, just as her father had taught her to check for weak spots before beginning any binding.

The stones were still cool as she knelt, arranging her gathered papers. She aligned the edges with practiced precision, despite the varying sizes and conditions. The makeshift signatures came together under her touch — not the fine volumes of her father's workshop, but something born of the same care and craft.

Meredith flipped through the church bulletins, her eyes scanning each sheet. Many had pristine blank backs, untouched by ink or water stains. She set these aside, building a small pile of usable paper. Within the pamphlets, she discovered extra blank pages — sheets that had escaped the printer's press entirely.

The paper quality varied. Some sheets felt thick and sturdy between her fingers, while others were thin and delicate. She sorted them by thickness, just as her father had taught her with the fine Italian papers in their workshop.

Her hands moved with practiced efficiency, folding the stronger sheets to create protective outer covers. The blank pages she grouped into signatures of four, aligning the edges with careful precision. The morning sun warmed her back as she worked, casting long shadows across her makeshift workbench of stone.

Using the thickest thread from what she had scavenged, she bound the signatures together. The needle pushed through easily, creating neat holes along the spine. She tightened each stitch with the same care she'd used on fine leather volumes, ensuring the binding would hold under use.

Some pamphlets she fashioned into simple folders, scoring the paper with her father's bone folder to create clean, sharp folds. These would protect loose papers from London's constant damp. Others she transformed into small notebooks, their blank pages waiting for words or figures.

The familiar motions calmed her racing thoughts. Each fold, each stitch connected her to the workshop on Paternoster Row. Her fingers remembered the rhythm — in and out with the needle, pull tight but not too tight, secure each gathering with a firm knot.

When she finished, a small collection of bound items lay before her. Simple, practical things born from discarded papers, but crafted with the same attention to detail that had marked every volume that left the Aldrich workshop. She ran her finger along one spine, testing the strength of her stitching. The binding held firm.

Meredith gathered her newly-bound pamphlets, cradling them like precious cargo. The paper edges caught the morning light, revealing the neat stitching that ran along their spines. Tommy stood beside her, scanning the bustling market square ahead.

"There's old Mr Finchley with his temperance speech," Tommy pointed toward a thin man in a worn black coat. "He pays fair, long as you catch him before the crowd thins."

Her heart hammered as she approached the street preacher. The sharp tang of unwashed bodies and rotting vegetables filled the marketplace. She clutched her work tighter, remembering how her father would present finished commissions to clients.

"Sir?" Her voice cracked. She cleared her throat and tried again. "Would you be interested in a pamphlet folder for your message? It will keep your notepaper neatly together?"

Mr Finch peered down at her work through wire-rimmed spectacles. His fingers traced the even stitching along the spine, and Meredith held her breath.

"Clean work," he muttered, testing the binding's strength. "How much?"

"Tuppence each, sir." The price stuck in her throat — in her father's workshop, such craftsmanship would have commanded shillings, not pennies.

He handed over sixpence for three pamphlets. The coins felt warm in her palm, earned through her own skill rather than charity or scrounging.

Tommy nudged her toward a cluster of political activists gathered near the fountain. Their red faces and passionate gestures had always intimidated her, but now she saw them differently — as potential customers.

A woman with a shock of grey hair waved her over. "What have you there, child?"

Meredith opened one of her pamphlets, demonstrating how the pages lay flat without breaking the spine. "Perfect for holding your speeches, ma'am. The stitching will last longer than single sheets."

The woman's weathered face broke into a smile. "Two dozen, if you can manage it by next week's rally."

Pride bloomed in Meredith's chest as she nodded, already calculating how many papers she'd need to collect. Her father's lessons, learned over years at his workbench, had given her more than just memories — they'd given her a way to survive.

18

A SMALL VICTORY

The morning crowd swelled around Meredith as she held up one of her bound pamphlets. "See how the pages stay together? No loose sheets to chase in the wind." Her voice carried across the marketplace with newfound confidence. A group of suffragettes gathered closer, examining her handiwork.

"The stitching allows it to lay flat when opened." Meredith demonstrated the feature, her movements precise and practiced. "Perfect for speeches or meeting notes."

From his perch near Watson's fruit stall, Tommy beamed. His new friend had transformed from the lost girl in the church doorway into a proper merchant. He watched her gesture animatedly as she explained her craft to potential customers, her earlier timidity forgotten in the familiar territory of bookbinding.

Banners snapped in the breeze above the market square, their bright colors casting shifting shadows across cobblestones. Vendors called out their wares while children darted between stalls, snatching fallen fruits. The air hummed with haggling and laughter.

Meredith noted how Mrs Watson slipped bruised apples to street children when her husband wasn't looking. Old Tom at the baker's stall turned a blind eye when small hands snatched day-old bread from his bins. But Mr Greene, the butcher, chased away any child who lingered too long near his shop.

She adjusted her route through the market accordingly, keeping clear of hostile vendors while positioning herself near the kinder ones. Their presence offered silent protection as she conducted her business, a dance of survival she was quickly learning to master.

A political speaker purchased six pamphlet folders – perfect for holding their own papers in -- praising the neat rows of stitching. "These will serve nicely for our next rally," he said, counting out coins into her palm.

∼

MEREDITH COUNTED the day's earnings as she settled into the familiar doorway of St. Michael's Church. The coins clinked against each other – seven pence from the suffragettes, eight from the political speaker, and three more from passersby who'd admired her craft. The weight felt reassuring in her palm.

Tommy slumped beside her, his legs stretched across the worn stone step. "You've got quite the business going." He pulled a half-loaf of bread from his coat. "Trade you some supper for the story of that fancy lady's face when you showed her the double-stitch binding."

The memory brought warmth to Meredith's cheeks. She dug into her pocket and broke off a piece of cheese she'd bought with her first sale. "Her eyes went wide as saucers when I explained how the pages wouldn't fall out."

"Just like your father taught you?" Tommy tore the bread in half, passing her the larger portion.

Meredith's fingers brushed the oilcloth bundle at her side. Inside, her father's bone folder and needles waited, ready for tomorrow's work. "Yes. Though he'd probably say my stitches are still too loose."

The setting sun painted the church walls in amber light. Around them, London's evening chorus swelled — cart wheels on cobblestones, shopkeepers calling final sales, children's laughter fading as they scattered home.

"We did well today." Meredith arranged the coins in neat stacks. "If I can find more paper tomorrow, maybe we could earn enough for meat pies by week's end."

Tommy nodded, crumbs dotting his shirt. "I know where they dump old ledgers behind the countinghouse. Paper's still good, just got numbers on one side."

Meredith clutched the coins tight, feeling their edges press into her palm. Each piece represented a step away from helplessness, a small victory won through the skills her parents had given her.

19
NO MORE

WINTER, 1847

Snow fell in thick curtains across London, transforming the streets into landscape of white. The bitter winter of 1847 had settled deep into the city's bones, turning the Thames to slate and coating the cobblestones in treacherous ice. Wind howled through the narrow alleys, carrying stray papers and the echoes of cart wheels through the white-shrouded streets.

Meredith pulled her threadbare coat tighter. Her fingers were red and chapped.

The doorway of St Michael's Church stood empty, a dark hollow in the whiteness. No Tommy appeared with his crooked grin and quick wit, no shared warmth of bodies huddled against the cold, no whispered stories to pass the endless hours. The space beside her felt vast, echoing with the absence of his voice.

"Bet I can nick three apples before old Watson spots me," she whispered to the empty air, mimicking Tommy's confident swagger. The words dissolved into the swirling snow, leaving only silence.

Her eyes burned as memories surfaced — Tommy teaching her to pick the safest sleeping spots, sharing stolen bread with a flourish as if presenting a feast, his laugh when she'd successfully sold her first batch of pamphlets. The cold seemed to reach deeper now, past skin and muscle, settling into her very core.

The wind picked up, driving needles of ice against her face. Meredith tucked her chin against her chest, remembering how Tommy would angle his body to shield her from the worst of the weather. But there was no shield now, no clever quip to make the bitter cold more bearable, no warm presence at her side.

Meredith huddled into the church doorway as memories of Tommy's last days crashed over her. His usual energetic movements had slowed first — the slight drag in his step as they'd searched for scraps, the tremor in his hands as he'd helped her bind pamphlets.

"Just tired," he'd insisted, voice hoarse. "Nothing a good night's sleep won't fix."

But sleep hadn't fixed it. The fever had come next, turning his skin to fire while he shivered under their shared blankets. She'd torn strips from her petticoat to cool his forehead, the fabric warming too quickly against his burning skin.

"Tell me about the books again," he'd mumbled one night, his words slurring together. "The ones with gold on the edges."

She'd described the gilt-edged volumes from her father's workshop, the way sunlight caught the gold and made it dance. Tommy had smiled, eyes glazed, and reached for her hand with clumsy fingers.

"You'll make beautiful books again someday," he'd said. "Proper ones, with leather and everything."

Reverend Mills had brought them soup, steam rising in the frigid air. Tommy had managed only a few spoonfuls before turning away, his usually voracious appetite gone. The bowl had grown cold between them as Meredith watched his laboured breathing.

The snow falling now reminded her of his final night — how the flakes had drifted down, so gentle and quiet, as Tommy's fever raged. She'd held his hand until dawn, whispering stories about magical bookbinders and brave street children who always found enough to eat. His fingers had grown cooler in her grip, his breathing softer, until his breathing had stopped altogether.

Now the empty space beside her felt vast and hollow. The snow continued its relentless descent, each flake a reminder of that terrible morning. No more shared warmth, no more clever plans for survival, no more whispered jokes in the darkness. The cold seemed to seep deeper into her bones without Tommy's presence to ward it off.

It wasn't fair. They had survived last winter, together. She and Tommy had huddled together in this very doorway, sharing scraps of bread and dreams of warmer days. That winter hadn't tried to freeze the marrow in her bones like this one.

Her stomach twisted with hunger. A year on the streets had hollowed her cheeks and stretched her skin tight across her bones. Her dress hung loose where it had once fit snugly, the fabric worn thin from endless wear. Without Tommy's quick wit and survival instincts, every shadow held new threats, every passing stranger a potential enemy.

The silver locket pressed cold against her chest, its weight a constant reminder of all she'd lost. Inside, her mother's wedding portrait smiled up at her, preserved behind glass like a pressed flower. The tools wrapped in oilcloth — her father's legacy — felt heavier with each passing day. What good were bookbinding skills to a girl who could barely keep warm?

She pulled her knees closer to her chest, trying to trap what little heat remained in her body. The muscles in her arms had wasted away, making even the simplest tasks a struggle. Tommy would have known what to do, where to find food, how to survive this bitter cold. But Tommy was gone, and she was alone with nothing but memories and treasured possessions that couldn't fill her empty stomach or warm her frozen fingers.

20
A WINDOW OF OPPORTUNITY

Frost crackled across the cobblestones as Meredith pressed herself against a large building's wall for shelter. She tried to remember the name of this place. Tommy had mentioned it once.

Thornfield Hall?

The cold seeped through her worn coat, numbing her fingers and toes, and casting any thought of names out of her mind. Above, the moon cast harsh shadows across the building's Gothic architecture, transforming familiar shapes into monstrous silhouettes.

Her teeth chattered as another gust of wind whipped around the corner. The temperature had plummeted far below freezing, turning her breath into white puffs that dissolved instantly in the bitter air. A tear froze on her cheek before she could brush it away.

Through an arched window, moonlight spilled across rows of leather-bound volumes in a personal library. The books stood in neat rows on mahogany shelves that stretched from floor to ceiling, their spines gleaming with gold tooling. The sight stirred something deep within her — a flicker of longing mixed with determination.

The library seemed to hold two faces in the moonlight. The warm glow of shelves laden with books beckoned like a siren song, promising warmth and the familiar comfort of leather and paper. Yet shadows lurked in the corners, and the massive oak door looked more fortress than entrance. The moonlight caught the brass handles, making them shine like watching eyes.

The library's dual nature — both welcoming and forbidding — matched the turmoil in her heart. Here was everything she loved, everything she knew, separated from her by glass and circumstance.

Meredith crept closer toward the library's largest window, her feet finding silent purchase on the frozen ground. Tommy's voice echoed in her mind: "Stay in the shadows, keep low, move slow." The alcove beneath the window swallowed her small frame as she knelt down.

The window was locked, but Tommy had taught her how to open locked windows from the outside.

From a hidden fold in her coat, she pulled out the metal strip she'd salvaged from behind Watson's fruit stall. Hours of careful filing against stone had transformed it into the thin tool Tommy insisted would "open any common lock." Her hands trembled, but not from cold.

"Gentle now," she whispered Tommy's words to herself, sliding the metal under the window's frame. She could see the latch, she just had to position the metal tool in such a way...

A clear click cut through the night air, sharp as breaking ice, as the latch fell away. Meredith froze, her breath caught in her throat. The sound seemed to echo across the empty grounds, though she knew it couldn't have carried far. Blood rushed in her ears as she waited, counting heartbeats like Tommy had taught her.

The window hinges groaned as Meredith eased it open. A rush of warm air embraced her, carrying the familiar scent of leather bindings and aged paper that made her throat tighten with memory. The library's atmosphere wrapped around her like one of Tommy's salvaged blankets, but infinitely more comforting.

Her frozen fingers tingled as she pulled herself through the window frame. The thick carpet muffled her landing, and she pressed herself against the nearest shelf, letting her eyes adjust to the darkness. Rows of books stretched upward, their spines catching glints of moonlight. The subtle creaks of settling wood and leather reminded her of late nights in her father's workshop.

The scent hit her fully now — morocco leather, paper, brass polish, and beneath it all, the sweet mustiness of old glue that spoke of countless hours of careful binding. Her father's tools seemed to hum against her side, as if recognizing their natural environment.

Moonlight poured through the towering Gothic windows, transforming the library into a silver-painted wonderland. The light caught the gilt edges of books, creating tiny constellations along the shelves. Shadows from the window's tracery cast elaborate patterns across the floor and walls, like illustrations from the fairy tale books her mother once read to her.

Between the shelves, reading nooks revealed themselves – deep leather chairs and small tables where countless hours had been spent in literary pursuit. The room breathed history and learning, each volume holding not just its printed words but the marks and memories of those who had handled them before.

Her heart thundered against her ribs as she took in the

vastness of the collection. More books surrounded her than she'd ever seen, even in her father's workshop during the busiest seasons. The moonlight through the Gothic windows painted silver paths between the shelves, creating an almost ethereal glow that made the library feel like a place outside of time.

21
THE LIBRARY

Meredith traced her fingers along the spines, each book whispering its history through leather and gilt. The familiar textures transported her back to the workshop, to days spent watching her father transform raw materials into works of art. Some bindings felt smooth as silk beneath her touch, while others bore the satisfying ripple of morocco grain that spoke of master craftsmanship.

Her father's bone folder pressed against her side as she moved deeper into the forest of books. The tools seemed to respond to their surroundings, as if awakening from a long sleep. She paused at a shelf of theological texts, their gold-tooled spines glowing in the moonlight. The precision of their finishing made her chest ache with memories of watching her father work late into the night, his hands steady despite exhaustion.

Between two massive folios, a gap caught her eye. There, on a bottom shelf, lay a Bible — but not just any Bible. Even in the dim light, she recognised the distinctive typography of a 1611 King James. The binding hung loose, its corners worn to the board, and several signatures had broken free from their cords.

The sight of such neglect stirred something deep within her. This was no ordinary volume, but a piece of history left to decay. Her fingers itched to repair the damaged spine, to restore the broken cords, to give the sacred text the dignity it deserved. The book's condition spoke to her like a wounded creature calling for help.

Kneeling beside it, Meredith ran her hand over the crumbling leather. Loose pages rustled beneath her touch, and the familiar smell of aged paper rose to meet her. The damage wasn't beyond repair — she could see that clearly now. The text block remained sound, despite its loose signatures, and though the binding had failed, the boards were intact beneath their worn covering.

Meredith unwrapped her father's tools from the oilcloth, the familiar weight of each piece grounding her in the moonlit library. The bone folder's worn surface caught the light, its patina speaking of years of careful use. Her father's voice echoed in her mind as she laid out the needles and thread with reverent care.

Her throat tightened as she gathered loose sheets of paper from a nearby desk and sorted through drawers until she found spare binding materials. Tears sprouted in her eyes that she quickly blinked away.

She settled cross-legged before the damaged Bible. Moonbeams streamed through the windows, casting pools of silver light across her workspace. The leather cover creaked as she opened it, examining the broken cords with practiced eyes.

Her fingers moved with inherited precision, threading the needle as her father had shown her countless times. "Mind the tension," she heard his voice whisper as she began the first stitch. The familiar rhythm of needle and thread through paper brought an ache to her chest, but her hands remained steady.

Each careful stitch felt like a conversation with her father. The bone folder smoothed each fold with the same dedication she'd witnessed in their workshop on Paternoster Row. Her father's techniques flowed through her movements — the careful spacing of the holes, the gentle tug of thread through signature — as natural as breathing.

The sacred text came alive beneath her touch, its pages whispering stories of her past. She worked methodically, letting muscle memory guide her through the familiar patterns of repair. With each passing moment, the Bible's spine grew stronger, its pages finding their proper place once more. The work consumed her, filling the hollow spaces grief had carved inside her chest.

22

LORD THORNFIELD

Lord Edmund Thornfield stood at his window, his reflection ghosting against the dark glass. The grounds stretched before him, winter-stripped branches reaching toward a sky heavy with snow. His deep blue eyes traced familiar paths where Charlotte had once walked, her parasol twirling as she meandered between the rose bushes she'd loved so dearly.

Fifteen years had passed, yet the hollow ache in his chest remained. The memory of her final moments, the midwife's urgent whispers, the sudden silence that followed — it all pressed against him like a physical weight. He touched the cold windowpane, remembering how Charlotte's delicate fingers had traced frost patterns there during their first winter together.

There was one place he could still feel her memory living on.

The library still held her presence. She'd arranged the theological texts by century rather than author, against the protests of three successive librarians. The leather-bound volumes stood in rigid rows, their gilt titles catching the lamplight like so many golden tears.

The grandfather clock in the hall struck midnight, each toll reverberating through empty corridors. Edmund's shoulders tensed at the sound. Time moved ever forward, dragging him away from those precious memories whether he wished it or not. Those books, once a shared passion between them, now gathered dust despite his best efforts. Charlotte had read to him here, her voice bringing ancient words to life as they sat before the fire. Now the chairs remained empty, the hearth cold.

He turned from the window, his footsteps echoing across the parquet floor, heading towards the library. With a heavy hand, he let the library's door creak open, and he stepped inside.

The shelves loomed around him, countless spines of morocco and calf, each one a reminder of evenings spent discussing theology and philosophy. Without her, they were just leather and paper, their wisdom locked away behind his grief.

Edmund's ears caught a whisper of movement from the depths of the library. The sound pulled him from his reverie — paper shifting against paper, the soft creak of binding. His eyes narrowed as he stepped away from the doorway.

Years of traversing these floors had taught him every quiet path. His boots made no sound on the carpets as he moved between the towering shelves.

There — between the theology section and the window alcove. A small figure hunched over one of the reading tables, little more than a shadow against the pale light. Edmund's hand tensed on the shelf beside him, but something held him back from calling out.

The street child's clothes hung in tatters, her dark hair

falling in tangles around her face as she worked. But those hands... Edmund found himself transfixed by their precise movements. Her fingers danced across the spine of what he recognised as the old King James Bible, the one Charlotte had always meant to have repaired.

The girl's movements spoke of years of training. She cradled the ancient binding with the same reverence Charlotte had shown their books, her stitches small and even as she secured loose pages back into place. The careful way she handled the worn leather brought a sudden tightness to Edmund's throat.

Without thinking, he took a step closer. The moonlight caught the silver of a needle as it flashed between her fingers, each stitch placed with practiced care. In the stillness of the library, he could hear her soft breaths as she concentrated on her work, completely unaware of his presence.

Edmund's breath caught as the girl's whispered words drifted through the stillness. "The cord needs replacing here... Father always said to mind the tension." Her speech carried the clear articulation of someone well-versed in literature, at odds with her threadbare dress and the grime streaking her face.

Her small fingers worked the needle with practiced precision, reminding him of Charlotte's own delicate touch when handling their most precious volumes. The girl's brow creased in concentration as she meticulously repaired each loose signature, her determination evident in every careful stitch.

A familiar ache bloomed in his chest. Here was a kindred spirit, someone else who understood the sanctity of books, who treated them as more than mere objects. Like him, she seemed to find solace in their pages, a refuge from whatever hardships had led her to break into his library on this bitter night.

Edmund's hand hovered near the shelf, caught between duty and fascination. He should call for the authorities, yet something held him back. The empty chairs in his library seemed to mock him — how many nights had he spent there alone, surrounded by volumes that now gathered dust? The books Charlotte had loved sat untouched, their spines growing stiff from disuse.

His gaze drifted to the girl's torn shoes, the thin shawl barely protecting her from the winter chill. What twist of fate had brought such refined speech and skilful hands to this state of destitution? The contrast between her evident education and current circumstances stirred something in him – a recognition of how quickly fortune's wheel could turn.

The warmth of his library, the security of his position, felt suddenly sharp against her desperate circumstances. Yet here she sat, not stealing or destroying, but repairing — preserving something precious with the same care he himself would have demanded.

23
CAUGHT RED-HANDED

Meredith's fingers trembled against the worn leather binding as she worked. The familiar motions of repair had lulled her into a false sense of security, making her forget the danger of her situation. A soft rustle of fabric shattered that illusion.

Her heart seized as a tall figure stepped from the shadows into the pale moonlight streaming through the windows. The movement sent her sprawling around as she scrambled to her feet. Her hair whipped across her face, partially obscuring her vision. Her chest tightened at the sight of the nobleman before her, his stern features carved in sharp relief by the silvery light.

Heat rushed to her cheeks as she pulled the newly repaired Bible close, pressing it against her worn dress. The weight of the book against her chest provided little comfort as her mind raced between the urge to bolt for the window and the desperate need to explain her presence. Her legs refused to move, frozen between these warring impulses.

"I mean no harm," the man said. His voice carried a gentleness that seemed at odds with his imposing height and formal bearing. He took a measured step toward her, and though his gaze held warmth, it also carried an intensity that pinned her in place. "My name is Thornfield. Lord Thornfield. This is my library."

Meredith studied him, noting the intelligence in his features and the way he observed her with more curiosity than anger. The knot in her throat began to loosen, though her fingers remained locked around the Bible. There was something in his manner that reminded her of the way her father used to examine particularly interesting bindings — careful, measured, analytical.

"How did you get in here, little one?"

"My father was a bookbinder on Paternoster Row." The words spilled from Meredith's lips before she could stop them. "He taught me everything – how to select the right leather, prepare the signatures, stitch the binding." Her hand brushed against the oilcloth bundle of tools.

Lord Thornfield's expression softened. He pulled a chair from the reading desk and sat, his height no longer looming over her. "Tell me more."

"Mother would read while we worked. Shakespeare and the Bible, mostly. The workshop smelled of leather and glue, just like..." Meredith's voice caught as she glanced around the library. "Like here."

Her fingers traced the repaired spine of the Bible. "When I saw this book, damaged and forgotten — I couldn't leave it. Books were our life, our home, until..." She swallowed hard. "The consumption took Mother first. Then Father worked himself to death on a commission. Twenty volumes for the Carter family."

Lord Thornfield leaned forward, his hands clasped together. "And after?"

"Mr Sands, our landlord, evicted me. I had nowhere else to

go." Meredith's chin lifted slightly. "But I kept Father's tools. Tommy — he taught me how to survive on the streets. Which doorways were safe, how to find food." Her voice dropped to a whisper. "The fever took him last week."

She held up the Bible. "When I found this, it felt like being home again. These books — they're more than just paper and leather. They're stories, memories. They deserve to be preserved."

Lord Thornfield's eyes held a depth of understanding that made Meredith's chest ache. He studied her work on the Bible with careful attention, noting the precise stitching and skilful repair of the worn corners.

"What is your name?"

"Meredith. Meredith Aldrich." Meredith paused a moment before remembering to add: "Sir."

Lord Thornfield. "Well, Miss Aldrich. You are clearly very skilled. Come with me."

24
AN OLIVE BRANCH

Meredith followed Lord Thornfield through the moonlit corridors, her father's tools clicking softly against her hip with each step. The nobleman's steady footfalls echoed against the polished floors, leading her past rows of portraits whose eyes seemed to track their progress.

He opened a heavy oak door, revealing a study lined with leather-bound volumes. A massive desk dominated the room, its surface neat save for a single inkwell and stack of papers. Lord Thornfield settled into the chair behind it, the leather creaking beneath his weight.

"Your skills are remarkable," he said, pulling a fresh sheet of paper toward him. The scratch of his pen filled the silence as he wrote. "I find myself in need of a junior maid. The position pays fifteen pounds annually."

Meredith's breath caught. Fifteen pounds. The sum danced in her mind. Her fingers brushed against the worn fabric of her dress, remembering the cold nights in church doorways.

"You would have quarters here, regular meals, and duties appropriate to your station." Lord Thornfield's deep voice carried a note of kindness she hadn't expected. "In return, I expect diligence and loyalty."

Tears pricked at Meredith's eyes. She blinked them back, refusing to let them fall. "Thank you, sir. I – I don't know how to express my gratitude." Her voice wavered but held steady. "I promise to work hard and prove worthy of your trust."

Lord Thornfield pushed the paper across his desk. The ink gleamed in the lamplight, still wet on the page. "Then we have an agreement, Miss Aldrich."

Meredith looked over of the agreement paper. "Why help me, sir? I broke into your home."

Lord Thornfield's gaze drifted to a small portrait on his desk. "My Charlotte had a gift for seeing worth in unexpected places. She would have recognised your skill, your dedication to preserving books." His voice softened. "Come, I'll show you to your quarters."

They climbed a narrow servants' staircase to the top floor. Lord Thornfield produced a ring of keys and unlocked a door, revealing a small room with a narrow bed and washstand. Moonlight spilled through a dormer window, catching dust motes in its beam.

"I apologise for the state of things." He swept his hand toward the unmade bed, a half-smile playing at his lips. "We weren't quite prepared for new staff at midnight."

Meredith stepped inside, clutching her father's tools to her chest. The room, despite its simplicity, felt like a palace after a year on the streets.

"The washroom is down the hall." Lord Thornfield pointed through the darkness. "Clean up and rest. I'll have Mrs Graves introduce you to the staff in the morning." He paused at the threshold. "Good night, Miss Aldrich."

The door clicked shut behind him, leaving Meredith alone in her new sanctuary.

25
MRS GRAVES

Sunlight streaked through the dormer window, waking Meredith from her first night in a real bed since the week after her father's death. The mattress, though thin, felt like Heaven compared to cold church steps. She smoothed her wrinkled dress, wishing she had something more presentable to wear.

A knock at the door made her jump. Lord Thornfield's voice carried through the wood. "Miss Aldrich? Are you decent?"

"Yes, sir." Meredith tucked her father's tools beneath the bed and opened the door.

Lord Thornfield stood in the hallway with a woman whose very presence seemed to fill the narrow space. Her eyes fixed on Meredith with such intensity that Meredith fought the urge to step back.

"Mrs Graves, this is Miss Aldrich, our new junior maid." Lord Thornfield's tone carried authority despite its gentleness.

The housekeeper's arms remained folded across her chest as she examined Meredith from head to toe. Her sharp nose wrinkled slightly at Meredith's shabby appearance. Everything about Mrs Graves spoke of precision and order, from her starched collar to her perfectly arranged grey hair.

"I see." Mrs Graves's voice cut through the air like a knife. Her lips pressed into a thin line as she continued her assessment. The woman's stern demeanour commanded respect, making Meredith stand straighter despite her fatigue.

"Miss Aldrich comes highly recommended for her skills with books," Lord Thornfield added.

Mrs Graves's eyebrows arched. "Books?" Her gaze swept over Meredith's worn clothing again. "And what experience does she have in household duties?"

Meredith's throat tightened. "I learn quickly, Mrs Graves."

Lord Thornfield's eyes softened as he gazed at Meredith. "She reminds me of Charlotte, you know. That same careful way with books." His voice caught on his late wife's name. "I leave her in your very capable hands, Mrs Graves."

He turned and strode down the corridor, his footsteps echoing against the wooden floors.

Meredith caught a fleeting change in Mrs Graves's expression — a shadow of tenderness crossed her stern features. The housekeeper's shoulders dropped slightly, and for a moment her rigid posture eased.

But the moment passed. Mrs Graves's spine stiffened, her face hardening back into its mask of authority. "Well then, Miss Aldrich. Let's see about getting you properly attired for your duties.

"Follow me." Mrs Graves turned on her heel, leaving Meredith to hurry after her down the servants' corridor.

Mrs Graves marched Meredith to a small washroom where a copper tub awaited. Steam rose from the water, and the scent of lavender soap tickled Meredith's nose. Her heart leaped at the sight — she hadn't had a proper bath since before her father's death.

"In you go. Scrub until your skin is pink." Mrs Graves's hands were rough but efficient as she helped Meredith out of her tattered dress.

The hot water enveloped Meredith like an embrace. Mrs Graves attacked her hair with soap, her fingers working through months of London grime. The housekeeper's movements were brusque, yet Meredith couldn't help but lean into the touch. Clean water sluiced over her head, carrying away the last traces of street life.

"Stand up." Mrs Graves wrapped her in a coarse towel. "Arms out."

A crisp white chemise slipped over Meredith's head, followed by stays that Mrs Graves laced with practiced hands. The black wool dress came next, its hem brushing Meredith's ankles. An apron, pristine and starched, completed the transformation.

"You'll need three of everything," Mrs Graves said, securing Meredith's cap over her damp hair. "One to wear, one to wash, one for Sunday best. Mind you keep them spotless."

As Mrs Graves took Meredith through to the servant's small dining space, Meredith caught glimpses of other servants passing by. A young maid with red cheeks pressed her face to the gap, only to be shooed away by Mrs Graves's sharp glare. Two footmen slowed their pace as they walked past.

"You rise at five sharp," Mrs Graves continued, ignoring the curious onlookers. "Breakfast at five-thirty. Morning prayers at six. Your duties begin immediately after." She adjusted Meredith's apron strings with quick, precise movements. "You'll serve at table, clean silver, dust the library shelves. Everything must be done to exacting standards."

Meredith nodded, still marvelling at the feel of clean skin and fresh clothes. A young kitchen maid hovering in the doorway caught her eye and offered a small wave before Mrs Graves's stern look sent her scurrying away.

∽

THE GRAND DINING room stretched before them, dominated by a mahogany table that could seat twenty. Gilt-framed portraits stared down from damask-papered walls. Meredith's hands trembled as Mrs Graves thrust a feather duster into them.

"Start with the chandelier. Every crystal must shine." Mrs Graves's eyes narrowed as Meredith gripped the duster's handle. "Not like that. Hold it properly – you're not sweeping streets here."

Heat crept up Meredith's neck. She adjusted her grip, but Mrs Graves clicked her tongue.

"The stepladder needs moving. Show me you can handle it without scratching the floor."

The wooden ladder weighed more than expected. Meredith's arms strained as she lifted it, careful not to let it drag. Each step felt like walking on eggshells under Mrs Graves's razor-sharp scrutiny.

"Now the chairs must be moved for proper cleaning underneath. Mind the legs don't scrape." Mrs Graves circled the table like a hawk. "Your hands are filthy – wash them before touching anything else."

Meredith looked down at her hands, calloused from over a year of street survival. The grime seemed ground into her skin despite her best efforts to clean them that morning.

"Yes, Mrs Graves." She headed for the door, but Mrs Graves's voice stopped her.

"And when you return, we'll discuss how to properly polish silver. Though I doubt you've ever handled anything finer than tin."

26
A FRIEND

Meredith's knees ached against the wooden floor as she scrubbed in tight circles, her raw hands gripping the brush. Three days of constant cleaning had left blisters across her palms, but she pressed on, determined to match Mrs Graves' exacting standards.

"You've missed a spot." Mrs Graves' shadow fell across the floorboards. "Over there."

Meredith shuffled backward, dipping her brush in the bucket. The water had grown cold and grey. She attacked the indicated spot with renewed vigor, though her arms trembled from exhaustion.

Mrs Graves glided past, her skirts rustling with precise movements. Each step carried purpose, every gesture efficient and graceful. She paused to adjust a candlestick on the mantle by a fraction of an inch, her reflection crisp in the polished brass.

"The silver needs attention after you finish here." Mrs Graves pulled back the heavy curtains, inspecting them for dust. "Every piece must shine for dinner service."

"Yes, Mrs Graves." Meredith's voice cracked from thirst.

In the kitchen, Meredith sorted through mountains of tarnished silverware. Her fingers worked the polishing cloth until each piece gleamed, while Mrs Graves supervised from her post by the doorway. The housekeeper's dark eyes missed nothing – a water spot on a soup spoon earned a sharp click of the tongue, a smudged fork handle prompted a withering stare.

"Faster," Mrs Graves commanded. "We haven't got all day."

Meredith's movements quickened, though fatigue made her clumsy. A butter knife slipped from her grip, clattering against the wooden table.

"If you cannot handle basic tasks with care, perhaps you're not suited for service after all." Mrs Graves' words cut deeper than any blade.

Meredith retrieved the knife with trembling fingers, fighting back tears as she resumed polishing. She wouldn't give Mrs Graves the satisfaction of seeing her cry. Instead, she focused on the silver's surface until she could see her own determined expression reflected back.

Meredith's muscles burned as she polished the last of the silver. A gentle touch on her shoulder made her start.

"Here." A maid pressed a warm roll into her hand, fresh from the kitchen ovens. "Eat quickly before Mrs Graves returns. I'm Martha by the way."

Martha's brown eyes crinkled with warmth as she kept watch at the doorway. The bread's heavenly scent reminded Meredith of Mrs Cooper's bakery, bringing a lump to her throat.

"Thank you," Meredith whispered, savouring each bite. "I'm Meredith."

"So I've heard! The maid that 'just appeared'! I remember my first week here." Martha grabbed a cloth and helped polish the remaining pieces. "Mrs Graves had me scrubbing floors until my hands bled."

Over the next few days, Martha appeared like clockwork — a guardian angel in servant's garb. She showed Meredith shortcuts through the manor's maze of corridors and taught her tricks for removing stubborn stains. When Meredith struggled with heavy loads of linens, Martha quietly took half the burden.

"You remind me of someone," Martha said one evening as they folded sheets together. "My brother James. He had your same determined look."

Meredith paused, noting the past tense. Martha's hands stilled on the fabric.

"The streets took him before I could help." Martha smoothed a wrinkle with practiced fingers. "I won't let that happen again."

When Mrs Graves questioned Meredith's whereabouts during afternoon tasks, Martha covered seamlessly. "She's helping me with the upstairs windows, ma'am." Or "I sent her to fetch fresh lavender for the linens."

After their shifts, they shared quiet moments in the servants' hall. Martha snuck plates of leftover shepherd's pie or bits of cake from the kitchen. They ate in comfortable silence, Martha's steady presence a balm to Meredith's aching heart.

One night, Martha's hands trembled as she set down her chipped teacup. "James was barely older than you when I lost him. The streets..." She traced the rim with her finger. "I had a position here, warm food, a bed. But I couldn't convince him to leave his friends. Pride, he said. Didn't want charity."

Meredith's chest tightened, memories of Tommy flooding back. The same stubborn independence, the same fierce loyalty to street companions.

"By the time I saved enough to help properly, the winter fever had taken him." Martha's voice cracked. "Found him in an alley off Cheapside. He looked so small, curled up there. Like when we were children."

Meredith reached across the table, covering Martha's hand with her own. The kitchen's warmth wrapped around them like a blanket, the copper pots gleaming in the lamplight.

"Tommy... A friend taught me to survive out there," Meredith whispered. "He showed me safe doorways, where to find food. Then the fever took him too."

Martha squeezed her hand. "We carry them with us, don't we? In everything we do. Whilst they watch down from Heaven."

27
DAILY CHORES

Meredith's cloth moved in slow circles across the silver serving tray, each stroke revealing her reflection in fragments. Dawn crept through Thornfield Hall's towering windows, casting long shadows across the dining room's polished oak floors. The morning light caught the crystal drops of the chandelier, scattering rainbow prisms across the white tablecloth.

She lined up the freshly polished pieces like soldiers — soup spoons, fish forks, dessert knives — each in its proper place. The familiar motions reminded her of arranging signatures before binding, the precise placement of each page crucial to the final product. Her father's voice echoed in her memory: "Everything has its place, just as every page has its gathering."

The silver sugar bowl required extra attention, its ornate patterns collecting tarnish in every crevice. Meredith's small fingers worked the polishing cloth into each curve and hollow, just as they once worked leather into the spine of a book. The metal warmed beneath her touch, like Morocco leather softening under her father's careful handling.

A beam of sunlight struck the newly polished surface, transforming the simple sugar bowl into something magnificent. It reminded her of the gilt edges they'd created together, how her father would hold up a finished volume to catch the light, making the gold leaf shimmer like captured sunshine.

Meredith's hands paused on a particularly stubborn water spot. The dining room's grandeur pressed in around her — the oil paintings in their gilt frames, the heavy damask curtains, the oriental carpet's intricate patterns. Yet her fingers itched for the familiar weight of a bone folder, the sticky resistance of hide glue, the satisfying crackle of fresh paper.

She lifted another piece from the silver chest — a gravy boat with handles curved like book clasps. The tarnish yielded to her methodical cleaning, revealing scrollwork that could have been lifted from one of her father's finest bindings. Each piece told its own story, like the books they'd rescued and restored together in their workshop on Paternoster Row.

Meredith set down the polishing cloth and flexed her tired fingers. The morning sun had climbed higher, warming the dining room's thick carpet. Her thoughts drifted to Lord Thornfield, who she'd glimpsed earlier striding through the hall with his usual purposeful gait. The deep lines around his eyes spoke of old griefs, particularly the loss of his wife Charlotte.

Charlotte's portrait hung in the house — a woman with kind eyes and a book open in her lap. Meredith had studied it during her cleaning duties, noting how Lord Thornfield would sometimes pause before it, lost in thought. The way he'd mentioned Charlotte's name when offering Meredith the position still echoed in her mind: Charlotte would have seen worth where others saw only circumstance.

The empty chairs around the massive dining table seemed to mock the absence of a child. In all her weeks at Thornfield, Meredith had never caught sight of Lord Thornfield's offspring. Once, she'd asked Mrs Graves about setting an extra place for dinner.

"That won't be necessary," Mrs Graves had snapped, her spine stiffening like a ruler. "Mind your assigned duties and nothing else."

Later, while they cleaned the silver together, Martha had leaned close to whisper the truth. "His daughter's terribly ill, poor thing. Stays in her room most days, up on the third floor." Martha's eyes had darted around to ensure Mrs Graves wasn't within earshot. "Only the most trusted servants are allowed to tend to her. Some say she's been sickly since birth, because of how difficult it was. As she entered the world, her mother left it you see..."

Meredith picked up another piece of silver, but her mind remained fixed on the mysterious daughter. The third floor's west wing was strictly off-limits to junior staff, its long corridor silent except for the occasional rustle of Mrs Graves's skirts or the quiet footsteps of senior maids carrying trays.

∼

MEREDITH CLIMBED the library's rolling ladder, feather duster in hand. The leather-bound volumes stretched endlessly above her, their spines a tapestry of burgundy, forest green, and midnight blue. She inhaled deeply — hide glue, paper, leather — scents that transported her back to Paternoster Row, to her mother reading Shakespeare while her father worked the finishing wheels.

Her cloth swept across the shelf edges, revealing gilt titles that winked in the morning light. A collection of Wordsworth caught her eye, reminding her of the dog-eared copy her mother had read from during summer afternoons. The familiar words had floated through their workshop, mingling with the tap-tap of her father's backing hammer.

Row by row, the dust yielded to her careful strokes. Each spine beneath her fingers told its own tale — some smooth and pristine, others cracked and peeling. In the corner, a stack of damaged volumes lay forgotten, their bindings split and signatures loose, and her fingers twitched with the urge to mend them.

A massive folio of botanical illustrations sagged against its neighbours, its spine partially detached. Meredith steadied it with gentle hands, noting how the cords had snapped one by one. The same breaks she'd learned to repair at her father's workbench, watching his skilled fingers weave new life into broken books.

The afternoon sun streamed through the windows, casting diamond patterns across the parquet floor. Meredith moved between the towering shelves like a ship threading narrow channels, each section holding new treasures. She paused before a shelf of poetry, remembering how her mother's voice had brought such verses to life in their small workshop, the words dancing between walls that now seemed a lifetime away.

28

THE BOOKBINDER'S APPRENTICE

Moonlight filtered through the library's windows as Meredith's footsteps whispered against the floorboards. She navigated between towering stacks, her father's tools wrapped in oilcloth pressed close to her chest. The household had settled into silence hours ago, leaving only the occasional creak of settling wood to accompany her midnight venture.

She chose a spot beneath the largest window where silvery light pooled across the reading table. The oilcloth rustled as she unwrapped it.

The damaged botanical folio lay before her, its broken spine a silent plea for attention. Meredith's hands moved with practiced precision as she gathered her supplies — thread, glue, and fresh mull she'd manage to source with Martha's help. The familiar scent of hide glue filled her nostrils as she worked it between her fingers, testing the consistency just as her father had taught her.

"Start with the spine, always the spine," she whispered to herself, hearing her father's voice in the words. Her needle slipped through the signatures with practiced ease, each stitch a testament to years spent watching Thomas work. The tactile sensation of thread pulling through paper brought tears to her eyes — not of sadness, but of connection to those countless hours in their workshop, the sound of her mother's voice reading Shakespeare mingling with the scratch of her father's tools.

The moonlight caught the silver gleam of her needle as it danced through the pages, weaving broken sections back together. In the quiet sanctuary of Lord Thornfield's library, surrounded by the ghosts of countless books, Meredith found herself truly at peace for the first time since leaving Paternoster Row. Her father's bone folder felt warm in her palm as she smoothed each repair, her movements guided by muscle memory and love of the craft. Her mother's silver locket felt cool and comforting against her chest, witnessing the work she was doing.

~

THE SOFT SCRATCH of her needle through paper filled the midnight silence. Meredith's fingers moved with practiced grace over the damaged spine of a leather-bound volume of pastoral poetry.

A whisper of slippers against wood made her freeze. Her heart thundered as she caught the reflection of candlelight in the window before her. She clutched her father's tools closer, preparing for discovery and dismissal.

"So you're the one." James Blake's gentle voice carried across the library. "I've been finding my damaged books mysteriously mended."

Meredith turned slowly, facing the elderly librarian. His steel-grey eyes studied her work with keen interest, none of the anger she'd feared. He moved closer, candlelight catching the silver in his beard as he bent to examine her repairs.

"These books need care, proper care," he said. "And it's been too long since I've had an apprentice worthy of teaching the finer points of restoration."

Meredith's shoulders relaxed as James settled into the chair beside her. His presence brought back memories of evenings spent watching her father work, the same quiet understanding hanging in the air.

"The bookbinder I learnt under taught me more than just binding," James said, his weathered hands ghosting over the leather. "My master believed in starting with the basics — even when I thought I knew better." He chuckled, the sound warming the midnight-dark library. "Spent three months just learning to fold signatures properly."

The memory of her father's similar lessons tugged at Meredith's heart. "My father always said the soul of a book lives in its stitches."

"Wise man, your father." James lifted one of Thomas's needles from her cloth bundle. "These are fine tools. Well-loved."

"They're all I have left of his workshop." Meredith traced the worn handle of the bone folder.

James nodded, understanding filling his eyes. "Come. Let me show you something." He retrieved a small volume bound in deep green morocco from a nearby shelf. "This was my first solo binding. See how the corners tell the story of my learning?"

Each evening after that, James waited in the library with candles lit and tools laid out. He guided her hands through French techniques she'd never seen before, showing her how to create intricate patterns in gold leaf and teaching her the secrets of different leather grains.

"The leather speaks to you," he said one night, helping her work a particularly stubborn piece of calfskin. "Listen to its whispers, feel how it wants to bend."

His gentle instruction reminded her of quieter days on Paternoster Row, but brought new joy too — the satisfaction of mastering complex patterns, of bringing fresh life to tired volumes.

29
BELONGING

Meredith looked over the delicate gold tooling on a repaired spine, admiring how James's techniques brought new elegance to her work, as she settled into her nightly ritual.

She pulled a worn copy of "Paradise Lost" from the stack of damaged books. Its spine hung loose, pages threatening to spill free. Moonlight streamed through the gothic windows, casting silver paths across her workbench. She didn't need a candle tonight.

Her needle dipped and rose through the signatures with practiced precision. James had taught her to angle the needle just so, creating stronger stitches that would hold for decades. The rhythm of the work transported her back to Paternoster Row, but the ache in her heart had softened. Here, surrounded by thousands of books, she felt her parents' presence in every stitch.

She incorporated the French pattern James had shown her last week — a delicate weave of threads that created an almost invisible strength beneath the spine. Her father's bone folder felt different in her hands now, smoother somehow, as if accepting these new techniques into its legacy.

The moon climbed higher as she worked, casting different shadows across the leather. She paused to admire how the light caught the grain – another detail James had taught her to consider. "Each hide tells its own story," he'd said, and she was learning to read those tales in the subtle patterns and markings.

A loose page slipped from another waiting volume, drawing her attention. The stack of damaged books seemed endless, but that thought filled her with joy rather than dread. Each broken spine and torn page was an opportunity to practice her expanding skills, to honour both her father's teachings and James' wisdom.

She lifted the newly bound "Paradise Lost," testing its weight. The cover moved smoothly under her touch, the spine holding firm as she opened it. Pride swelled in her at how the pages lay flat, evidence of proper tensioning – a technique she'd struggled with until James showed her the correct pressure to apply.

A creak from the floorboards sent Meredith's heart racing. She froze, needle suspended mid-stitch, and peered into the shadowy corners of the library. The moonlight cast strange shapes across the shelves, turning harmless books into looming figures. Her fingers trembled as she set down her tools.

The sound faded, but her pulse refused to slow. Every night brought the same fear — discovery by Mrs Graves meant losing not just her position, but this sanctuary of leather and paper that had become her salvation. She'd survived the streets, yet the thought of being cast out of Thornfield terrified her more than any cold doorway ever had.

The leather beneath her fingers grounded her. Its smooth

surface, warmed by her touch, reminded her of countless hours in her father's workshop. She picked up the bone folder again, its worn handle fitting perfectly in her palm. The soft scrape of tool against hide echoed her father's movements, each practiced stroke a testament to generations of craft.

Still, doubt crept in like London fog. A street urchin playing at nobility, that's what Mrs Graves would say. The silver locket at her throat felt heavy with the weight of her deception. But as she traced the gold tooling on her latest binding, the precise lines and elegant curves told a different story. This wasn't pretence — this was who she had always been.

Meredith stepped back from the workbench, studying the row of restored volumes. Each repair represented more than mended pages and strengthened spines. They were bridges between her past and present, between the girl who lost everything and the young woman who had found her way back through craft and kindness.

The moonlight caught the gold leaf she'd applied using James's techniques, making it shimmer like hope itself. Lord Thornfield's kindness, Martha's friendship, James' mentorship — these gifts had transformed her parent's legacy into something new and wholly her own. In these quiet hours, surrounded by the fruit of her labour, Meredith felt the deep satisfaction of belonging.

30
A NEW SEASON

SUMMER, 1848

Meredith leaned against the windowsill of the servants' quarters, breathing in the sweet summer air that drifted up from Thornfield's gardens. The morning sun painted London's rooftops in shades of gold, so different from the grimy winter that had driven her to break into this very house. Six months had transformed those desperate nights into something she scarcely recognized.

Below, Martha crossed the courtyard with a basket of fresh linens, her quick steps and cheerful whistle carrying up through the open window. Even Mrs Graves' sharp voice calling out instructions to the footmen held a familiar comfort now.

Meredith smoothed her clean apron, fingers lingering on the starched fabric. The calluses from her days in the workshop remained, but they'd found new purpose in polishing silver and arranging delicate china. Her hands knew their place here

— whether wielding a feather duster by day or a needle in the secret hours of night.

The silver locket at her throat caught the morning light. She'd stopped hiding it beneath her collar weeks ago, and none of the other servants questioned its presence. Like the books she tended in the library, she'd become part of the household's story — perhaps an unusual chapter, but one that belonged all the same.

A breeze carried the scent of roses from the garden, mingling with the familiar smell of leather and paper that seemed to permeate every corner of Thornfield. The same wind that had once cut through her thin coat on London's streets now brought only the promise of another day among people who, if not quite family, had become something more than strangers.

She watched a pair of sparrows dart between chimney pots, their wings catching the light. Strange how the same city that had shown such cruelty could now seem so beautiful. The morning bells of St Michael's rang in the distance, no longer a reminder of Tommy's absence but a melody that marked her place in this new world.

31
ALICE THORNFIELD

Lord Thornfield's footsteps echoed through the library as Meredith arranged the morning's dusting supplies. His tall figure cast a shadow across the polished floor, and she turned to face him with a quick curtsy.

"How have you found these past six months, Miss Aldrich?"

"Wonderful, sir. I cannot express my gratitude enough." Meredith's fingers brushed the silver locket at her throat, a habit that surfaced whenever she felt moved by emotion.

"You've proven yourself quite capable." He paused by the window, his hand resting on the leather-bound volume she'd repaired the previous night. "There's something of Charlotte in you — my late wife."

Lord Thornfield's eyes softened as he spoke of Charlotte, though his posture remained straight as a ruler. "I have a new task for you, one I believe you're uniquely suited for."

He led her up the manor's grand staircase, past portraits of stern-faced ancestors, to a corridor she'd never entered during her cleaning duties. The scent of lavender grew stronger with each step.

The chamber door opened to reveal walls adorned with lilac paper, its delicate pattern catching the morning light. A girl sat propped against pillows in a window seat, her pale face turned toward a book in her lap.

"Alice, my dear. This is Miss Aldrich."

Meredith's gaze swept across the room, taking in the towering bookshelves that lined every wall. Leather bindings in various states of wear filled each shelf — some pristine, others well-loved with cracked spines that spoke of countless readings. Tales of adventure and romance, histories and poetry collections stood like silent friends keeping watch over their young mistress.

Alice looked up from her book, her light blue eyes bright with interest despite the obvious fatigue in her face. The lavender sachets hanging near her bed mixed with the musty scent of old paper, creating an atmosphere both refined and comforting.

Alice quickly slipped the book she was reading under her covers, but Meredith would have been able to recognise that book anywhere; a well-worn copy of "Jane Eyre" that Meredith knew from her own mother's readings. The sight tugged at her heart, reminding her of afternoons in the workshop when Elizabeth's voice had brought stories to life.

"Father says you know about books." Alice's voice carried a gentle warmth despite its weakness.

"I learned bookbinding from my father." Meredith stepped closer, noting how the morning light caught the gold tooling on the spines of nearby volumes.

Lord Thornfield cleared his throat. "Miss Aldrich has shown remarkable dedication in her duties. I believe she would make an excellent companion for you during your convalescence — that is, if you approve."

Alice's face brightened. "Oh yes, Father. Anyone who treats books with such care must have a gentle soul."

Meredith's chest warmed at the girl's words. Lord Thornfield outlined her new responsibilities — bringing fresh linens, preparing herbal teas, maintaining the chamber's cleanliness, and most importantly, keeping Alice company during her long hours of bed rest.

The following days found Meredith settling into a rhythm of care. She learned which herbs soothed Alice's chest — thyme and chamomile steeped just so — and how to arrange the pillows to ease her breathing. The physical tasks gave purpose to her hands, reminding her of the precise movements required in bookbinding.

Alice's cough echoed through the chamber, harsh against the morning quiet. Meredith rushed to her side with a fresh handkerchief, supporting her shoulders until the fit passed. The light in Alice's eyes dimmed with each episode, her usual brightness clouded by exhaustion.

"Thank you," Alice whispered, her breath still uneven. "The others — they're kind, but they don't stay. They can't bear to watch."

Meredith adjusted the lavender sachet near Alice's pillow, remembering how her own mother had suffered. The familiar sound of labored breathing filled the room, driving Meredith to action. She opened the curtains wider, letting sunshine spill across the floor, and selected a volume of poetry from the nearest shelf.

"Shall we read together?" Meredith asked, determined to bring light back to those blue eyes. "Your father mentioned you enjoy Wordsworth."

32
BONDING

Meredith pulled the worn copy of "Jane Eyre" from beneath Alice's pillow, her fingers tracing the familiar leather binding. The afternoon sun cast long shadows across the lilac wallpaper as she settled into the window seat beside Alice.

"Have you reached the part where Jane stands up to Mrs. Reed?" Alice's eyes sparkled with an intensity that belied her frail frame.

"That's my favourite scene." Meredith opened to the dog-eared page. "Mother used to say Jane had fire in her soul."

Alice leaned closer, her shoulder brushing against Meredith's. "Father thinks it's improper reading for a lady. He caught me once and lectured for an hour about suitable literature."

Meredith glanced at the door before lowering her voice, "Then we'll have to be clever about it."

They huddled together over the pages, whispering about Jane's courage in the face of cruelty. Alice gasped at each twist.

"Sometimes I feel like Jane," Alice confessed, picking at a loose thread on her blanket. "Trapped by circumstances beyond my control. These four walls become my Lowood Institution."

Meredith thought of her own confinement in poverty, the invisible walls that had hemmed her in on London's streets. "But Jane never stops fighting for more."

Alice's fingers found Meredith's hand. "Tell me again about binding books with your father. About your mother reading Shakespeare while you worked."

The words flowed easily now, memories of leather and glue mixing with the lavender-scented air. They lost themselves in stories within stories — Jane's determination echoing in tales of Meredith's survival, Alice's dreams of health and freedom weaving through their shared readings.

Meredith always made sure she never told Alice about her time on the streets, about the cold nights huddled in doorways or scrounging for scraps. She had learned from Martha, during their quiet conversations in the servant's quarters, that it would have been deemed improper what Lord Thornfield did by taking in an urchin and so Meredith had made sure to keep that part of her story private from everyone, even Alice. The shame of that desperate year clung to her like a shadow, and she feared that revealing such truth might strain the delicate friendship they had built, might make Alice see her differently despite her kind heart.

33
REAL STRENGTH

Meredith watched Alice's delicate hands tremble as she lifted them above her head, counting breaths just as Dr Bennett had instructed. The afternoon light streamed through the window, casting a golden glow across the lilac walls of Alice's chamber.

Meredith's heart quickened at the memory of Dr Bennett's first visit to Alice's chamber. She'd frozen in place that day, recognising his familiar face from those dark months when he'd treated her mother. The doctor had paused in the doorway, his medical bag clutched in one hand, and Meredith's world had tilted sideways.

Her hands had trembled as she'd arranged Alice's pillows, certain her past would come spilling out. Dr Bennett knew everything — her mother's death, her father's decline, the workshop on Paternoster Row. He'd seen her family crumble piece by piece.

But then he'd done something remarkable. His eyes had met hers for just a moment, and he'd offered the smallest wink before turning to Lord Thornfield.

"Ah, and this must be the new maid you mentioned." Dr Bennett's voice had carried the perfect note of polite interest. "A pleasure to make your acquaintance, Miss Aldrich."

He'd extended his hand as if they were perfect strangers, as if he hadn't once pressed a cool cloth to her mother's fevered brow or prescribed cod liver oil that they couldn't afford. Meredith had grasped his hand, feeling the same gentle strength that had once checked her father's pulse.

Relief had washed over her like a spring rain. In that moment, she'd understood — Dr Bennett would keep her secret. He recognized what Lord Thornfield had done by taking in a street child, knew the delicate balance of her position in the household.

Now, watching Alice practice her breathing exercises, Meredith silently thanked the doctor for his discretion. His kindness had protected not just her position, but the friendship blooming between her and Alice.

"One more time," Meredith encouraged, supporting Alice's back. "Dr. Bennett says these movements help your lungs grow stronger."

Alice's face flushed with effort, but she managed a smile. "It's easier with you here. Before, the exercises felt like punishment."

Meredith adjusted the pillows behind Alice's back, remembering how she had done the same for her mother during her final days. But where those memories brought pain, helping Alice filled her with purpose.

"Tell me about the fairy gardens again," Alice requested between careful breaths. "The ones you invented while binding books."

"They lived in the leather grain," Meredith said, guiding Alice's arms in a gentle circle. "Each piece of morocco held entire worlds if you looked closely enough. Father showed me how to spot the patterns."

Alice giggled, the sound brightening the room like sunshine after rain. "I see them too now, in the bindings of my books. Yesterday, I found a castle in the spine of 'A Midsummer Night's Dream.'"

The exercises, once a dreaded chore, transformed into a game. They invented stories for each movement — reaching arms became fairy wings, gentle twists were dancing princesses. Even on days when Alice's strength waned, their shared imagination carried them through.

"You make everything into an adventure," Alice said, her breathing steadier now. "Even these horrible exercises."

Meredith helped Alice settle back against the pillows. "That's what friends do. They turn the ordinary into something special."

Meredith felt warmth spread through her chest. In these quiet afternoons, she found pieces of herself she thought lost forever on London's streets. Alice's chamber became a haven where stories and laughter chased away the shadows of illness.

One afternoon, Alice traced her finger along the window pane, following a raindrop's path down the glass. "What's it like out there? Really like, I mean. Not just what I see from up here."

Meredith's hands stilled on the leather-bound volume of Wordsworth she'd been holding. The question struck something deep inside her — memories of bitter winds and empty stomachs warred with the scent of fresh bread from Mrs Cooper's bakery and the bustle of Paternoster Row.

"It's..." Meredith chose her words carefully. "It's not always as romantic as books make it seem. But there's beauty too — the way fog rolls off the Thames at dawn, or how the gaslights make everything glow golden at dusk."

"I wish I could see it all." Alice's voice carried a yearning that made Meredith's heart ache. "Sometimes I dream of walking through London, visiting bookshops, hearing street musicians play. Just... being free to go wherever I please."

"Your world may seem small now, but look how much you've accomplished within these walls." Meredith moved closer to Alice's chair. "You speak French better than anyone I know, and your understanding of literature — the way you find meanings others miss. That's its own kind of freedom."

Alice turned from the window, her pale face flushed. "But you've lived it, Meredith. You've faced real challenges and survived them. I just... exist here, protected from everything."

"Courage isn't measured by how far your feet can carry you." Meredith thought of how Alice faced each day with a smile despite her struggles to breathe. "It's in how you face what life gives you. The way you never let your illness dim your spirit — that's real strength."

"Do you really think so?" Alice's eyes brightened with unshed tears.

"I know so. Your heart holds more adventure than most people who've traveled the world. And the way you share that with others, through your kindness and wisdom — that's rarer than any street performance or London fog."

34
WINTER CHILL

WINTER, 1848

Meredith noticed the changes as winter's chill crept through Thornfield's halls. Alice's cough returned, deeper than before, and her breathing exercises grew more laboured. Where once they'd spent hours inventing stories about the patterns in book bindings, now Alice often dozed off mid-sentence, her face pale against the pillows.

The familiar fear that had haunted Meredith during her mother's illness rose again. She watched Alice's chest rise and fall during afternoon readings, counting each breath like she used to count stitches in leather bindings.

"Perhaps we should rest," Meredith said one particularly difficult day, closing their copy of 'Pride and Prejudice' as Alice's coughing interrupted Mr. Darcy's first proposal.

Alice shook her head, her fingers clutching the blanket. "No, please. I want to know what Elizabeth says next."

But her voice had grown thin, like paper worn too fine, and dark circles shadowed her eyes. The autumn sun that once painted their afternoons golden now seemed to wash all colour from Alice's face.

Their shared moments of joy became scattered between longer stretches of silence. Some days, Alice couldn't summon the strength to sit up, let alone participate in their usual conversations about literature and life. Meredith arranged Alice's pillows, adjusted blankets, and tried to ignore how her friend's nightdress hung looser with each passing week.

During one of Alice's better days, they managed to resume their fairy garden stories, but Alice's imagination wandered, her usual sharp wit dulled by fever. Meredith's heart clenched as Alice struggled to remember details of their previous tales.

Where once they'd spent hours discussing Jane Austen's heroines, now Meredith often sat alone beside Alice's bed, watching her friend drift in and out of consciousness. Each ragged breath reminded Meredith of those final days in the workshop on Paternoster Row, when her mother's cough had echoed against walls lined with unfinished books.

∼

MEREDITH PULLED another leather-bound volume from her apron pocket. She'd spent the early morning hours selecting stories that might lift Alice's spirits – tales of triumph over adversity, of friendship conquering all odds.

"I thought we might try something different today." She settled into her usual chair beside Alice's bed. "Remember how you said Jane Eyre's spirit gave you strength?"

Alice's pale face brightened. "Did you find another story like that?"

"Several." Meredith arranged the books on Alice's coverlet, their spines forming a rainbow of possibilities. "Each heroine faces her own battles, just as we do."

"Tell me about them?" Alice pushed herself up against her pillows, and Meredith noticed how her nightdress hung loose at the shoulders.

"This one's about a girl who builds a secret garden." Meredith traced the gilt lettering. "She transforms not just the garden, but everyone around her through sheer determination."

They spent the afternoon diving into new worlds, Alice's cough momentarily forgotten as they discussed Mary Lennox's transformation from bitter child to garden enchantress. When Alice's energy flagged, Meredith shifted to reading aloud, her voice carrying them through hidden gardens and secret doors.

"Sometimes I feel like Mary," Alice whispered during a pause. "Trapped inside these walls. But then you bring these stories, and it's like finding my own secret garden."

The winter wind rattled the windows, but inside Alice's chamber, their shared warmth created a sanctuary. Meredith poured them both tea from the waiting pot, and they held their cups like precious treasures.

"To friendship," Alice said, lifting her cup with trembling hands. "And to all the heroines who showed us how to be brave."

"To us," Meredith replied, her throat tight with emotion. "The heroines of our own story."

Their cups clinked softly, the sound barely audible above the howling wind outside. In that moment, Meredith felt the strength of their bond — two girls finding courage in each other's company, building their own garden of hope amid winter's chill.

35
THE NEPHEW

Crisp winter air seeped through the windows of Thornfield Library, carrying whispers between towering mahogany shelves. Meredith paused her dusting, her cloth frozen mid-stroke across leather spines. The heavy oak door creaked open.

Sunlight streamed through stained glass, casting rainbow patterns across the figure who stepped inside. This had to be Mr Philip Ashworth, Lord Thornfield's nephew.

His tall frame filled the doorway, his light brown hair catching the morning rays like a halo. His waistcoat, perfectly tailored in deep burgundy, spoke of wealth and privilege that made Meredith's maid's uniform feel coarse against her skin.

Her heart skipped. Mrs Graves' words from breakfast echoed in her mind: "Lord Thornfield's nephew arrives today. You're not to speak to him unless spoken to directly." The housekeeper's stern face had pinched with displeasure. "And even then, keep your answers brief."

But there was something in Philip's bearing that defied such rigid rules. His hazel eyes held a warmth that reminded her of summer afternoons in her father's workshop, when sunlight would dance across fresh-bound books. He moved with an easy grace through the library, trailing his fingers across book spines in a way that spoke of genuine reverence for their contents.

Meredith clutched her dusting cloth tighter, willing herself to become invisible among the shelves. Yet curiosity bloomed in her, spreading like ink across parchment. Here was someone who touched books the way she did —not as mere objects, but as vessels of wonder.

Philip moved deeper into the library, his steps purposeful as he approached the theological section. His fingers traced the gilt lettering on leather spines, pausing at Augustine's "Confessions." He pulled the volume free, its pages rustling as he thumbed through well-worn passages.

Meredith watched from behind a shelf as he mouthed words silently, his brow furrowed in concentration. The way he handled the book echoed how her father would examine a text before binding — gentle yet certain, reading not just the words but understanding the soul of the work.

He replaced Augustine only to retrieve Aquinas, then Calvin, creating a small stack on the reading desk.

Meredith was drawn closer to where Philip sat. Her mother's voice echoed in her memory, reading passages from these same texts while her father worked. She knew these books intimately — not just their bindings, but their contents, absorbed through countless hours of readings and discussions in their workshop.

Philip's finger traced a passage about faith and works, his lips moving in silent debate with the text. Meredith's hands itched to point out the corresponding arguments in Tyndale's works just two shelves away. But Mrs Graves' warning held her back, the invisible wall between servant and the master's nephew as solid as the oak shelves surrounding them.

Yet something in his earnest study called to her. The way his shoulders tensed when he encountered a challenging passage, how he'd pause to consider before turning each page — these weren't the actions of someone merely fulfilling an obligation. Here was a mind wrestling with truth, just as she had so often done during her mother's readings.

Meredith's fingers trembled on her dusting cloth. The books called to her like old friends. Philip's furrowed brow as he studied Augustine's words mirrored her own countless moments of contemplation.

She stepped from behind the shelves, her heart thundering against her ribs. "Might I assist you in finding anything, sir?"

Philip looked up, surprise flickering across his features. "I'm searching for Augustine's thoughts on divine grace." His voice carried none of the dismissive tone she'd come to expect from the upper class.

"There's a particularly relevant passage in book ten." The words slipped out before she could stop them. "He speaks of grace as a gift freely given, not earned through merit."

His eyes widened. "You're familiar with Augustine?"

"My mother sometimes read theological works while my father bound them." Heat crept into her cheeks. "The words found their way into my heart as surely as the leather found its way onto the boards."

"That's fascinating." Philip shifted in his chair, making space at the reading desk. "What are your thoughts on his view of predestination compared to free will?"

Meredith sank into the offered seat, forgetting for a moment the vast social gulf between them. "Augustine wrestles with this, much as we all do. He speaks of God's sovereignty while maintaining human responsibility — like two threads woven together in the same cloth."

"An apt metaphor." Philip's eyes lit up. "Have you considered how this relates to Aquinas's natural law theory?"

Their discussion flowed from Augustine to Aquinas, each point building naturally upon the last. The familiar rhythms of theological debate reminded Meredith of evenings in the workshop, when her mother would pose similar questions while binding proceeded.

"Speaking of divine inspiration," Philip said, "what's your view on Shakespeare? His work seems touched by something beyond mere human creativity."

Meredith's eyes lit up. "Shakespeare captures the heart's truths in ways theology sometimes misses. Those passages in 'The Tempest' on dreams, simply wonderful! He even has Caliban — this seemingly monstrous being — bring such dreams to life with beautiful poetry."

"I have to admit," Philip blushed slightly, "I have not read as much of Shakespeare as I would like to. I have not yet read 'The Tempest', but it shall be the next thing I read!"

Meredith couldn't help but blush herself.

Philip's face flushed suddenly. "I've been terribly rude. Here we are discussing literature and theology, and I haven't even introduced myself. I'm Philip Ashworth."

"Meredith Aldrich." She dipped her head slightly. "I work here at Thornfield."

"Meredith?" Recognition flickered across his features. "You're the one who keeps Alice company?"

"Yes, though she's with Dr Bennett this morning." Meredith glanced at her abandoned dusting cloth. "Mrs Graves assigned me some cleaning while Alice has her examination. Which I should return to, before she notices my absence."

"Of course." Philip smiled warmly. "I've just returned from

Oxford, and I must say, this has been the most engaging discussion I've had since leaving. Even my professors couldn't draw such elegant parallels between Augustine and Shakespeare."

Meredith felt heat rise in her cheeks as she stood, smoothing her apron. "You're too kind, sir. I simply speak from what I've learned through years of listening."

"Please, call me Philip. And thank you for the conversation. I look forward to continuing our discussion another time."

36
DISCUSSIONS

The library's familiar scents of leather and paper greeted Meredith each morning as she dusted the shelves, but now they carried a new anticipation. Philip appeared like clockwork, his footsteps on the marble floor announcing his arrival before he rounded the corner with an armful of books.

"Cousin Alice tells me you've been reading Jane Eyre together," Philip said one morning, settling into his usual chair. "Though I hear you keep it hidden from Uncle Edmund."

Meredith's hands stilled on the leather spine she'd been cleaning. "Miss Thornfield finds comfort in Jane's story. Your uncle might not approve, but it brings her such joy."

Their theological discussions expanded to include Alice, who delighted in having her cousin back. Her pale face brightened whenever Philip joined their afternoon readings, bringing fresh perspectives to their literary debates. Even on her weakest days, Alice insisted on participating, propped up against pillows while Meredith and Philip acted out scenes from Shakespeare.

"Do Mr Rochester's voice again," Alice would beg, her eyes sparkling despite her fatigue. "Philip does it perfectly."

The hours slipped by in Alice's lilac-wallpapered chamber, sunlight streaming through tall windows as they shared passages from their favourite works. Philip brought books from his own collection – worn copies of Milton and Donne that sparked new conversations.

"Father says you're here more than at Oxford nowadays," Alice teased her cousin one afternoon, while Meredith arranged flowers by the window.

Philip's response carried a warmth that made Meredith's fingers tremble on the stems. "Oxford's libraries seem rather dull compared to the discussions we have here."

Between readings and debates, Meredith caught glimpses of Philip watching her — when she adjusted Alice's blankets or shared insights about a particular passage. His gaze held none of the dismissive quality she'd come to expect from the gentry. Instead, she found genuine interest and something deeper that made her heart flutter against her better judgment.

During these conversations, Meredith felt most like herself — not a maid, not a former street child, but simply someone who understood the power of words bound in leather and gold. Philip's presence brought warmth to the library that reminded her of happier days in her youth, when knowledge and craft intertwined seamlessly.

In the library, James Blake would busy himself with cataloging whenever Philip appeared, though Meredith caught the old librarian's knowing winks. Between the towering shelves, she and Philip found sanctuary among the books, their whispered conversations dancing between theology and literature.

"Your understanding of these texts is remarkable," Philip said one afternoon, gesturing to a passage in Aquinas. "You speak of them as if you've studied at University yourself."

Meredith's fingers traced the leather binding of the volume before her. "My mother read extensively while my father worked. The discussions they shared shaped my understanding of these works."

Sunlight filtered through the high windows, casting long shadows from the shelves that surrounded them like protective walls. Their corner of the library became their own world, where station and class melted away beneath the shared ideas and passionate debate.

Their discussions flowed naturally, moving from theological concepts to poetry and back again, their voices kept low in deference to the library's sanctity.

Meredith held up Augustine's "Confessions" as she recited from memory: "'You have made us for yourself, O Lord, and our hearts are restless until they rest in you.'" The familiar words flowed easily, echoing her mother's voice from years of readings in their workshop.

Philip leaned forward in his chair, his hazel eyes bright with interest. "You speak it as if you've lived with these words your whole life."

"Mother believed great works should be remembered, not just read." Meredith adjusted the book on its stand, remembering the rhythm of her mother's voice mixing with the tap of her father's tools. "She would read while Father worked, asking me to repeat passages until they became part of me."

A small smile played at Philip's lips as he watched her handle the delicate pages. "Most people I know at Oxford merely memorise texts for examinations. But you — you understand them, feel them."

Meredith moved to return the volume to its shelf, aware of his gaze following her movements. Even in her maid's uniform, she carried herself with the quiet dignity her mother had instilled. "These words kept me company during difficult times. They became more than just passages to recite."

"I've noticed." Philip's voice softened. "You speak of Aquinas' virtues as if you've walked alongside them, tested them against life itself."

Heat rose to Meredith's cheeks as she recalled the cold nights when Tommy's lessons in survival had tested every virtue she'd learned. Yet here she stood, still holding fast to the wisdom her parents had shared, still finding strength in bound pages and remembered verses.

"That's what makes your understanding so remarkable," Philip continued. "You've lived these philosophies, not just studied them. It shows in every discussion we have."

37
A THREAD TO THE PAST

Moonlight streamed through the library's windows as Meredith worked alongside James Blake. Her fingers moved with practiced precision across the leather binding before her, applying gold leaf to the spine of a worn volume of Marlowe's works.

James adjusted his spectacles, watching her technique. "Steady now. Let the pattern flow naturally." He nodded as she completed the line of decorative tooling.

Meredith cleaned her tools. Working in the library at night brought her closest to memories of the workshop on Paternoster Row.

"Young Mr. Ashworth seemed particularly engaged in discussion with you this afternoon," James remarked, organising the finishing wheels on their rack. "Quite the scholarly debate."

Heat crept up Meredith's neck. She focused intently on wiping her tools clean, avoiding James's knowing look. "He's very kind to visit Alice so often. His cousin benefits greatly from the company."

James hummed softly, a gentle smile playing at his lips as he returned to his work. The quiet of the library enveloped them once more, broken only by the soft sounds of their tools against leather and the occasional rustle of pages being sewn.

Meredith's hands stilled as she lifted the next volume from the mending pile. The worn leather binding, its corners softened with age, bore the distinctive cross-hatched pattern her father had favoured. Her heart quickened as she opened the cover.

There on the flyleaf, written in her younger hand: "Property of Meredith Aldrich, Paternoster Row." Below it, she'd sketched a small bird in flight — her childhood mark in all her books.

Her fingers trembled as she turned the pages of 'The Tempest'. Margin notes in faded ink traced her thoughts from years past. The paper held the ghost of her mother's voice, reading Prospero's lines on winter evenings while her father worked.

James looked up from his workbench. "Found something interesting?"

"This was mine." Meredith touched a dog-eared corner where she'd marked her favourite passages. "From our workshop. Father bound it for my tenth birthday." She traced the familiar tooling on the spine, remembering how her father had let her choose the pattern herself.

The book's journey from their humble workshop to Thornfield's grand library struck her — how many hands had held it, how many shops and auction houses had it passed through? Like her, it had wandered far from Paternoster Row to find its place here.

A pressed flower fell from between the pages — a dried violet had been tucked into Ariel's song. The brittle petals crumbled at her touch, but the purple stain remained on the paper, marking the passage: "Nothing of him that doth fade, But doth suffer a sea-change, Into something rich and strange."

Meredith swallowed hard and laid the book on James's workbench. Her father's bone folder felt heavy in her palm as she gathered her tools. The leather needed careful attention where it had split at the joints, and several signatures had come loose from their sewing.

James placed a steadying hand on her shoulder. "Take your time with this one."

She nodded, unable to speak past the tightness in her throat. The familiar motions of repair work anchored her — checking the binding structure, testing the cords, examining where the leather had worn thin. Her father had taught her to approach each damaged book like a patient needing care.

James guided her through the French technique for reinforcing the spine, showing her how to blend the new work seamlessly with her father's original binding. The leather responded to her touch as she worked glue into the joints, her fingers remembering every lesson from the workshop.

A tear threatened to fall as she reached the section containing her mother's favourite speech. Meredith turned her face away, letting the droplet land on her apron instead of the page. James quietly handed her his handkerchief.

"Your father's work was exceptional," James said softly, examining the original tooling. "See how precisely he matched the pattern at the corners? That takes real skill."

The praise for her father's craftsmanship helped steady her hands as she carefully reattached the loosened signatures. Each stitch felt like connecting another thread to her past, preserving not just the book but the memory of evenings spent learning at her father's workbench.

38
A HEARTFELT GIFT

Meredith's heart drummed against her ribs as she held out 'The Tempest' to Philip.

"Do you remember our first conversation here? About Shakespeare?" Her fingers traced the familiar leather binding. "I wanted to share this with you."

Philip set aside his theological text. "Is this—?"

"From my father's workshop." Meredith's voice softened. "He bound it for my tenth birthday. Every marking, every note inside — they're memories of evenings spent listening to my mother read while he worked."

The book trembled slightly in her hands as she opened it to show him the inscription. "See? This was our address on Paternoster Row. And here—" She pointed to the small sketched bird. "That was my mark in all my books."

Philip's eyes widened as he accepted the volume, handling it with reverent care. "These annotations..." He turned the pages slowly, studying her childhood thoughts scrawled in the margins. His finger hovered over a faded violet stain marking Ariel's song. "You've captured such wonderful insights here."

"Mother always said 'The Tempest' was about forgiveness and redemption." Meredith watched as Philip discovered her detailed notes about Prospero's journey from bitterness to grace. "Each time we read it, I found new meanings to explore."

Philip's expression softened as he examined the cross-hatched pattern on the spine, the precise tooling at the corners. "Your father's craftsmanship was extraordinary." He paused at a page dense with her younger self's observations. "And these notes — they're remarkable."

Heat crept up Meredith's neck. "Mother always encouraged us to find our own meaning in the text."

"Would you..." Philip cleared his throat. "Perhaps we could make this a regular occurrence? There are so many volumes here worthy of exploration, and I'd value your perspective on them."

The leather of 'The Tempest' creaked as Philip closed it carefully. "We could meet here in the evenings, after your duties. Choose a new book each week, share our thoughts."

Meredith's pulse quickened. Here was someone who saw beyond her station, who valued her mind as much as her practical skills. "I'd like that very much."

"Excellent." Philip's smile brightened his entire face. "Shall we start with this, 'The Tempest'? We could begin tomorrow evening, if you're free? After Alice has gone to sleep."

A warmth bloomed in Meredith's chest, different from anything she'd felt before. Here in this library, surrounded by beloved books, she'd found someone who understood both worlds she inhabited — the practical and the intellectual.

"Tomorrow evening would be perfect."

39
A NEW SPRING

SPRING, 1849

Spring swept through London like a painter's brush, daubing colour across the dreary cityscape. Meredith watched from her window as Philip strode up the path to Thornfield Hall, his figure catching the late afternoon light that poured through the glass. The sun transformed the usually somber room into a golden sanctuary. She rushed off to meet him in the library.

Philip's now familiar smile greeted her as he entered. They settled into their usual corner, where theological texts mingled with poetry on the shelves around them.

Their discussions had deepened over the months, weaving between complex religious philosophy and shared memories. Philip's laughter filled the space between the shelves as Meredith recounted her mother's dramatic readings of the Psalms.

Alice's recovery seemed to mirror the season's renewal. Her cough had eased with the warmer weather, allowing her to sit up longer during their reading sessions. Philip never arrived without something to brighten her day — a pressed flower, a curious mechanical toy, or a book with particularly beautiful illustrations.

"Look what I found," Philip said, producing a worn copy of Donne's poetry. "Your notes in the margins rival the text itself."

Meredith traced the familiar pages. "These were difficult ideas to grasp when I first read them. Father encouraged me to write down every question, every thought."

They exchanged volumes like confidences, each dog-eared page and penciled note revealing another layer of understanding. Their theological debates now flowed naturally into personal revelations, creating a tapestry of shared knowledge and trust.

40
LADY ASHWORTH

Lady Catherine Ashworth paced across the carpet in her private sitting room at Ashworth Manor, her fingers trailing along the carved mahogany desk where Philip's letters from Oxford had once arrived like clockwork. These days, her son's presence at home grew scarcer with each passing week. The spring sun cast long shadows through the floor-length windows, highlighting the empty chair where he should have been studying his theological texts.

A tea service sat untouched on the side table, the china growing cold as she tracked Philip's latest excuse. "Researching at Uncle Edmund's library again," he'd claimed, but his collar had been askew and his eyes had held that dreamy distance she'd come to despise.

The maid. Always mentions of the maid.

"She has the most fascinating perspective on Augustine's Confessions," Philip had said at breakfast, butter knife suspended mid-air. "Her father apparently bound theological works, and she—"

Catherine's hand clenched around her letter opener. The

girl had wormed her way into Edmund's household through some tale about bookbinding, and now she dared to discuss theology? With her son?

Through the window, Catherine watched as Philip's figure appeared at the gates, returning far later than proper hours dictated. Even from this distance, she caught the spring in his step, the looseness in his shoulders that spoke of pleasant company rather than serious study.

Her reflection in the window glass showed the tightening of her jaw, the way her green eyes narrowed to chips of jade. Edmund had always been soft-hearted, too willing to see the best in people regardless of their station. But Catherine knew better. She'd worked too hard, sacrificed too much to maintain their family's position in society.

The letter opener clicked against the desk as she set it down. This situation required more than maternal concern—it demanded action. Someone needed to investigate this girl's background, to expose whatever scheme she'd concocted to rise above her station.

∼

CATHERINE SWEPT into Edmund's study, where her brother sat hunched over estate ledgers. Afternoon light caught the silver threading through his dark hair, making him look older than his years. The room carried that familiar mustiness that had always reminded her of their father.

"The household seems to be running smoothly," she began, trailing her fingers along the spines of nearby books. "Though I noticed some... changes in the staff."

Edmund barely glanced up. "Mrs Graves maintains excellent order."

"Yes, particularly that new maid — the one Philip

mentions. What was her name? Meredith?" Catherine watched her brother's face for any reaction. "Such an unusual name for a servant."

"She tends to Alice." Edmund's pen scratched across the page. "Does good work."

"But where did she come from? Surely Mrs Graves checked her references?" Catherine's voice remained light, though her fingers pressed harder against the leather bindings.

Edmund set down his pen with a sigh. "I trust my judgment in these matters, Catherine."

The dismissal in his tone only strengthened her resolve. Later that afternoon, she cornered Mrs Mills, wife of the local vicar, during their weekly tea. The woman's tongue loosened easily enough with the right encouragement.

"A street urchin, they say," Mrs Phillips whispered behind her cup. "Though no one knows for certain. Appeared out of nowhere in the dead of winter."

Catherine's cup clinked against its saucer. The thought of such a creature sharing theological discussions with her son, polluting his mind with common ideas—her Norman blood practically boiled. Through the parlour window, she caught sight of Philip crossing the garden with that familiar distracted air about him, no doubt fresh from another encounter with the girl.

A lineage that traced back to William the Conqueror would not be undermined by some guttersnipe with pretensions above her station. Catherine set down her cup with careful precision, her mind already forming plans.

41
EDMUND'S DILEMMA

Edmund stood at the library window, watching Philip's retreating form cross the courtyard below. The young man's confident stride reminded him of Charlotte — the same determined set of shoulders, the same purposeful gait. His sister Catherine's words from earlier that day pricked at his conscience like thorns.

He traced the leather spine of the King James Bible Meredith had repaired that winter night. The girl's skill with a bone folder and needle had saved more than just the book. In those careful stitches, he'd recognised something of Charlotte's reverence for literature, her belief that true worth lay beyond the constraints of birth and station.

The candlelight caught his reflection in the window glass. Dark circles shadowed his eyes, evidence of sleepless nights spent weighing duty against conscience. Catherine's investigation into Meredith's past troubled him more than he cared to admit. The girl's time on London's streets, her association with known thieves — these facts could destroy Philip's prospects.

Yet Edmund couldn't forget how Meredith had transformed Alice's chamber from a sickroom into a sanctuary of stories and laughter. His daughter's health had improved markedly since Meredith had taken over care for his Alice, her episodes of melancholy lifting like morning mist.

He sank into Charlotte's old armchair, its worn velvet still holding the shape of her absence. What would she have counselled? Charlotte had defied her own family to marry him, believing love could bridge the gulf between a nobleman and a gentleman's daughter turned governess.

"The heart knows its own truth," she used to say.

But Edmund's position demanded more than just matters of the heart. As head of the family, he bore responsibility for its reputation and future. Philip's prospects, Alice's security — all could be jeopardised by Meredith's background.

His mind drifted to opening the library door that fateful winter night. Such a simple thing to have altered so many lives. Now he wondered if his compassion then might prove Philip's undoing.

42
A LOOMING SHADOW

Lady Ashworth arranged the tea service with precision, each china piece placed just so on the mahogany table. Family portraits loomed from gilt frames, generations of Ashworths watching her every move. The parlour's heavy curtains filtered the afternoon light, casting shadows across Mr Frederick Pinkerton's weathered face as he settled into the wing-backed chair across from her.

"You understand the delicacy of this matter, Mr Pinkerton." Catherine poured the tea with steady hands. "My son's future hangs in the balance. This... person has wormed her way into our household through Edmund's misplaced charity."

Pinkerton's pen scratched against his leather-bound notebook. His green eyes flickered between the page and Catherine's face, missing nothing.

"The girl spends hours with Philip in the library, filling his head with theological discourse far beyond her station. She appeared during the winter of '46, claiming to be a bookbinder's daughter." Catherine's lip curled. "Yet she provides no proof, no references. Even Mrs Graves reports suspicious behaviour — sneaking about at night, whispering with other servants."

Steam rose from the untouched tea before them as Catherine detailed every observation: the late-night meetings, the shared books, the growing influence over Alice. Her voice dripped with disdain as she described Meredith's educated manner of speech, so incongruous with her position.

Pinkerton nodded, his pen never stopping. "Rest assured, Lady Ashworth, I shall be thorough in my inquiry. My methods have unveiled many such... deceptions in the past."

"Excellent." Catherine straightened her spine. "I trust you'll maintain absolute discretion. The Ashworth name must remain untarnished."

"Of course, my Lady." Pinkerton closed his notebook with practiced efficiency. His mind already churned with possibilities — workhouse records to examine, streets to canvas, witnesses to question. This investigation promised to be most illuminating.

∽

MEREDITH RAN the feather duster across the leather spines, each book a familiar friend under her touch. Evening sun streamed through the library's tall windows, casting long shadows across the carpet. The books surrounding her wrapped around her like a warm blanket, yet her shoulders remained tense.

"My mother used to read these same volumes." Philip's voice broke through her concentration. He stood in the doorway, a worn copy of a large book in his hands. "Though I doubt she understood them half as well as you do."

Her cheeks warmed at the compliment. She kept her eyes on the shelves, maintaining the proper distance expected between a maid and a gentleman. "Your mother sounds like a remarkable woman."

"She was. Is." Philip crossed to the window seat. "Though she can be... protective. Especially since Father passed."

Meredith's hands stilled on the spine of a theological text. The weight of her past pressed against her like a physical thing. Street dirt under her nails. Tommy's fever-bright eyes. The crack of ice under thin shoes.

"Tell me about growing up at Oxford," she said, forcing lightness into her voice. The duster moved again, methodical strokes across gilt lettering.

Philip's face brightened. "The gardens in spring were magnificent. Row boats on the river. Late nights debating philosophy by candlelight." He paused. "You would have loved it there."

The words hung between them, heavy with possibility and peril. Meredith focused on the familiar motions of cleaning. Each sweep of cloth against leather grounded her in the present moment, in this sanctuary of books and learning she'd found at Thornfield.

"Perhaps someday you'll see it yourself," Philip added softly.

Meredith's heart fluttered at the thought, even as her mind warned against such dreams. She had found peace here — meaningful work, Alice's friendship, evenings spent discussing literature. The risk of losing it all loomed like a shadow at the edge of her vision.

43
PINKERTON

Frederick Pinkerton tucked his leather-bound notebook into his coat pocket and adjusted his hat against the morning drizzle. The cobblestones of Paternoster Row glistened beneath his feet as he made his way past shop fronts, marking each potential source of information.

Mrs Cooper's bakery caught his eye first. The aroma of fresh bread drew him inside, where he purchased a meat pie and struck up a casual conversation.

"Terrible business with the Aldrich girl," he said, counting out coins. "Heard she was living rough for a time."

Mrs Cooper's hands stilled on the counter. "Poor lamb lost both parents. Thomas worked himself to death, he did. The girl had nowhere else to go. I thought she could stay with me, but..." Pinkerton politely averted his gaze as Mrs Cooper wiped a tear from her eye.

At Cedar's Printing House, Mr Cedar recalled the family. "Quality work, the Aldrichs. Thomas could make a book sing. The girl learned his trade well enough."

Each conversation added another layer. The butcher

mentioned seeing her with "that Wilson boy" near St Michael's Church. The fruit seller remembered them scrounging for bruised apples. A washerwoman spoke of missing linens around the same time.

In his office that evening, Pinkerton spread his notes across his desk. The candlelight flickered across pages filled with testimonies — some painting Meredith as a skilled craftsman's daughter fallen on hard times, others hinting at darker associations.

Tommy Wilson's name appeared repeatedly. Street vendors described him teaching other children to pick pockets, though none directly implicated Meredith. Still, their connection troubled him. Several merchants reported missing small items during the year the pair frequented their shops.

The reverend at St Michael's offered a different perspective. "They slept in my doorway through the worst of winter. The girl bound prayer books for pennies — fine work too. But that Tommy..." He shook his head. "Always looking for an easy way."

Pinkerton's quill scratched across fresh paper as he documented each detail. Lady Catherine would be particularly interested in the Wilson boy's reputation for theft, even if Meredith's own hands appeared clean.

Pinkerton pushed back from his desk, the weight of his findings pressing against his conscience. The candlelight cast dancing shadows across the collection of testimonies — each one a potential nail in Meredith's coffin. His eyes scanned his findings on Tommy Wilson, a history of petty theft and street survival that now threatened to destroy the life Meredith had built.

A crisp sprint draft whistled through his office window. He pulled his coat tighter, remembering the warmth in Mrs Cooper's voice when she spoke of the girl. The baker's words echoed in his mind: "She had her father's skill and her mother's heart."

The sharp contrast between Meredith's past and present struck him. Here was a child who had learned to pick locks alongside Tommy Wilson, yet now spent her evenings discussing theology with Lord Thornfield's nephew. The same hands that once collected discarded papers from gutters now repaired precious volumes in one of London's finest libraries.

Lady Catherine would seize upon Tommy Wilson's criminal connections. She'd paint Meredith as a corrupting influence, ignoring the desperate circumstances that had forced a young girl onto London's unforgiving streets.

Pinkerton's throat tightened as he imagined Meredith's inevitable dismissal. The thought of her returning to those cold doorways and empty alleyways twisted in his gut.

He shuffled through his notes again, finding Dr Bennett's testimony about Thomas Aldrich's dedication to his craft, the respect the man had earned among London's bookbinders. Such a heritage, reduced to a scandal because of a year spent on the streets.

His quill hovered over the final report. Lady Catherine expected a thorough account of Meredith's misdeeds, and Pinkerton was a man of his word.

44
WHISPERS

Meredith's fingers trembled as she polished the brass doorknobs in the east wing corridor. The familiar motion brought little comfort today. Something had shifted in Thornfield Hall, like a shadow passing over the sun.

The cook's assistant Emma darted past, averting her eyes. The kitchen maid Martha, usually warm and chatty, busied herself with reorganising the already neat linen cupboard when Meredith approached.

In the servant's hall, conversation died the moment she entered. Footman George cleared his throat and gathered his cleaning rags. The scullery maid Sarah suddenly remembered urgent duties elsewhere.

Unspoken words hung over her as she worked. With every passing hour, she caught another servant watching her with a mix of curiosity and something else — was it suspicion?

During the afternoon tea service, Mrs Graves scrutinised her every move with narrowed eyes. The housekeeper's mouth pressed into a thin line as Meredith arranged the china cups.

"That will be all," Mrs Graves said, her voice carrying an edge Meredith hadn't heard before.

In the kitchen, Cook's spoon clattered against a pot when Meredith entered. The woman's face flushed as she turned away, speaking in hushed tones to her assistant. Their words dissolved into silence at Meredith's approach.

Her hands shook as she arranged silverware for dinner service. The familiar patterns of spoons and forks brought no peace today. Instead of the usual satisfaction in their gleaming surfaces, she saw only distorted reflections of her own worried face.

The tools of her father's trade, hidden in her quarters, seemed to call out to her. Would they brand her a thief if they knew about her nighttime binding work? Would her carefully constructed world crumble if they discovered the truth about Tommy Wilson and the streets of London?

Meredith climbed the familiar stairs to Alice's chambers, her heart lighter with each step despite the day's whispers. The warm glow from Alice's room spilled into the hallway, a beacon of comfort in the growing darkness.

Alice sat propped against her pillows, her face brightening at Meredith's entrance. "I've been waiting for you. Come sit with me."

The simple kindness in Alice's voice nearly broke Meredith's composure. She crossed to the chair beside the bed, smoothing her apron with trembling hands.

"Something's troubling you." Alice reached for Meredith's hand. "The servants have been whispering all day. I heard them outside my door."

Meredith's throat tightened. "What did they say?"

"I couldn't hear them well enough to make out anything specific." Alice's fingers squeezed Meredith's. "Just that there are rumours about you. But listen to me carefully — I don't care what they are. You've been more of a sister to me than anyone else in this house."

Meredith blinked back tears, remembering all their shared afternoons of reading, their quiet conversations, the way Alice had never once looked down on her despite their different stations.

"Whatever comes, I'll stand by you," Alice said, her pale face set with determination. "I won't let anyone drive you away. Father listens to me, and I'll make him understand that you belong here."

The simple declaration, spoken with such fierce loyalty, broke through Meredith's careful walls. A tear slipped down her cheek as Alice pulled her into an embrace, the gesture worth more than any words of comfort.

45
REVELATIONS

Meredith's heart hammered against her ribs as she stood among the other servants in Thornfield's drawing room. The afternoon sun cast long shadows through the tall windows, painting Lady Catherine's face in harsh angles as she gripped a leather folder to her chest.

The rustle of starched aprons and shuffling feet filled the tense silence. Martha's shoulder pressed against Meredith's, a small gesture of solidarity that did little to calm the storm in her chest — it was only yesterday that Martha had avoided Meredith's eye. Even Mrs Graves, usually so composed, twisted her hands together.

Lord Thornfield sat in his high-backed chair, one hand resting on the armrest, his expression unreadable. Philip stood behind him, his usual warmth replaced by rigid formality. The space between them stretched like an uncrossable chasm.

Lady Catherine's silk dress whispered across the carpet as she positioned herself before her brother. Her lips curved into something between a smile and a sneer as she surveyed the assembled household. A man Meredith didn't recognise —

though his bearing suggested authority — lingered near the doorway, his keen eyes missing nothing.

"Brother," Lady Catherine's voice cut through the silence. "I've called this gathering to address a matter of grave importance to our family's reputation." She tapped the folder with one gloved finger. "Mr Pinkerton has conducted a thorough investigation into the background of a certain... individual currently employed in this household."

The folder's leather binding caught the sunlight, and Meredith's throat constricted. It reminded her of the ones her father used to craft, though this one held not stories of adventure or romance, but the dark chapters of her past she'd fought so hard to leave behind.

Lady Catherine's eyes found Meredith's across the room, sharp as steel. "Some of us, it seems, have been harbouring a wolf in sheep's clothing."

Lady Catherine's voice dripped with venom as she opened the folder. "I've discovered that this... girl," she jabbed a finger towards Meredith, "has been engaging in unauthorised activities in the library at night. Not content with her position as a maid, she's taken it upon herself to handle precious volumes without permission."

Meredith's fingers curled into her palms, nails biting flesh. She watched Lord Thornfield's face, searching for any trace of the kindness he'd shown that first night.

The silence stretched as Lord Thornfield turned his gaze to Meredith. "Is this true? Have you been working in my library at night?"

Meredith's throat tightened around the words, but she refused to lie. Her father had taught her better. "Yes, sir. I've been repairing damaged books."

"Repairing?" Lady Catherine scoffed. "More likely destroying priceless volumes with her common hands."

James Blake stepped forward from his position near the bookshelves, his weathered face flushed. "If I may speak, my lord. Miss Aldrich's work is exceptional. Her technique rivals that of the finest bookbinders in Edinburgh. I've been teaching her advanced methods, and her skill—"

"You've been teaching her?" Lady Catherine's voice cracked like a whip. "A servant?"

Philip moved forward, colour rising in his cheeks. "Mother, if you'd only see—"

"Silence." Lady Catherine's hand shot out, stopping Philip mid-step. Her fingers trembled as she turned a page in the leather folder. "If her unauthorised tampering with valuable books isn't enough to convince you, brother, perhaps you'd like to hear about her time on the streets of London?"

Meredith's heart lurched. She felt every eye in the room bearing down on her, but none burned quite like Philip's. He looked... She couldn't tell, and that was the worst thing.

Lady Catherine's lips curved into a cruel smile as she smoothed the page before her. "It seems our little bookbinder had quite the education before arriving here – in theft and deception."

Lady Catherine's silk rustled as she withdrew several papers. "This creature we've welcomed into our home spent a year living on the streets of London, consorting with thieves and pickpockets." Her lip curled. "In particular, a known criminal by the name of Tommy Wilson."

Tommy's name in Lady Catherine's mouth felt like a physical blow. Meredith's vision blurred as she remembered his final fevered moments, his hand cold in hers as the snow fell.

"A street urchin, playing at being a proper servant. And even then, she's not been very proper, has she?" Lady Catherine's words cut through the shocked silence. "Associating with criminals, breaking into homes — yes, brother, I know how you came to find this supposed 'lost lamb'. Mr Pinkerton's investigation has been *very* thorough."

Gasps rippled through the assembled staff. Martha's shoulder withdrew from Meredith's, the small comfort vanishing. Through her tears, Meredith saw Philip's face drain of color, his hands gripping the back of his uncle's chair until his knuckles whitened. Lord Thornfield's expression darkened like storm clouds gathering over the Thames, his jaw clenched tight as he stared at the folder in his sister's hands.

Meredith's world spun as Lady Catherine's accusations hung in the air. The leather folder's contents had ripped open wounds she'd thought long healed, exposing her past like fresh cuts.

"If Meredith must go, then I shall go too!"

The voice pierced through the drawing room's thick tension. Meredith's heart stopped as she turned to see Alice standing in the doorway, her nightdress wrinkled and her face flushed with effort. Alice's thin fingers gripped the doorframe, her chest heaving with exertion from the descent downstairs.

Lord Thornfield leapt from his chair. "Alice, you shouldn't be out of bed—"

"No, Father." Alice's voice carried a strength Meredith had never heard before. Her small fists clenched at her sides as she straightened her spine, though her legs trembled beneath her. "I won't stay silent while you cast out the only person who's made me feel truly alive."

The gathered servants shifted uncomfortably. Mrs Graves pressed her lips together, her usual stern expression wavering. Even Lady Catherine seemed taken aback, her grip on the damning folder loosening slightly.

Alice took a shaky step forward, her bare feet pale against the dark carpet. "Meredith has shown me worlds beyond these walls through books and stories. She's given me courage when

I had none. If her past makes her unworthy to stay, then I'm unworthy too."

The silence that followed felt like a physical weight. Meredith watched as colour rose in Alice's cheeks — not the fever-flush she'd grown to fear, but the healthy glow of righteous anger. For a moment, the sickly girl transformed into something fierce and untouchable, her mother's daughter indeed.

Meredith's vision blurred with tears as she watched Alice sway slightly. The girl's nightdress hung loose around her thin frame, yet her stance held more strength than Meredith had ever witnessed. This was no longer the bedridden child who struggled to sit up — this was Charlotte Thornfield's daughter, standing against injustice with fire in her eyes.

The familiar ache of guilt twisted in Meredith's chest. She'd tried so hard to protect Alice from the harsh realities of her past, to be worthy of their friendship. Now Alice risked her health to defend that very friendship, and Meredith couldn't find the words to stop her.

Lady Catherine's leather folder drooped in her hands as she stared at her niece. The assembled servants shifted their weight, eyes darting between Alice and their master's. Even Mrs Graves's stern facade cracked, her hand rising to her throat as she watched Alice tremble with the effort of standing.

Alice's declaration hung in the air like a challenge to the very foundations of Thornfield Hall. The girl who had once whispered secrets beneath blankets now spoke truth to power, her voice carrying the weight of innocence and wisdom combined. She saw past the street urchin, past the maid's uniform, to the heart of who Meredith truly was.

Meredith's hands shook as she fought the urge to rush forward and support Alice's weakening frame. The girl's chest heaved with each breath, her bare feet curling against the carpet's pile. The effort of standing, of speaking out, painted her cheeks with dangerous colour. Yet her eyes remained bright and determined, fixed on her father's face with unwavering conviction.

This was friendship stripped bare of society's rules — pure, honest, and desperately fragile. In Alice's stand against propriety, Meredith saw the truth of their bond reflected back at her. No longer was she alone facing Lady Catherine's accusations. Alice had chosen her side.

Meredith's heart skipped as Dr. Bennett stepped forward from the corner of the drawing room. His presence, usually a harbinger of worry over Alice's health, now brought an unexpected warmth to her chest. His dark coat rustled as he moved to stand between her and Lady Catherine.

"My lady, if I may speak." Dr Bennett's voice carried the same gentle authority he used when tending to Alice's worst breathing spells. "I've had the privilege of knowing the Aldrich family for many years. Thomas Aldrich was not just a craftsman, but a man of principle who served London's literary community with distinction."

Lady Catherine's lips parted in protest, but Dr Bennett continued, his calm tone unwavering. "I treated Elizabeth through her illness. Meredith's parent's dedication to their craft, their daughter, and their community never faltered. The same dedication I see in Meredith's care for Alice.

"Miss Aldrich's presence has done more for Alice's health than any tonic I could prescribe. The improvement in her breathing, her spirits — these are not coincidences." Dr Bennett's eyes met Lord Thornfield's. "As your family's physician and a member of the Royal College, I stake my professional reputation on vouching for her character."

The servants stirred, whispers passing between them. Mrs Graves's stern expression softened slightly, and Martha's shoulder pressed against Meredith's once more. Even George, the footman who'd been avoiding her gaze all week, nodded slightly.

"A street child is hardly—" Lady Catherine began, but her words lacked their earlier venom as several of the older servants murmured in agreement with the doctor's assessment.

Dr Bennett stood firm, his presence as steady as it had been all those nights he'd tended to Meredith's mother. "The measure of a person's worth lies not in their circumstances, but in their actions. Meredith Aldrich has proven herself through her work, her care, and her character."

From her position among the servants, Meredith noticed movement in the corner of the drawing room. Mr Stanley Harrison stepped forward, his stocky frame casting a long shadow across the carpet. His presence surprised her — she remembered him as her father's rival, often competing for the same commissions on Paternoster Row.

"Pardon the interruption," Harrison cleared his throat, adjusting his waistcoat with weathered hands. "I had actually come this morning to discuss a matter with Lord Thornfield and seem to have stumbled into quite a situation." A few nervous chuckles rippled through the room, breaking the tension slightly.

Harrison's eyes fell on the leather-bound volume sitting on the side table — the fourteenth book of the Carter commission, her father's final work. He moved towards it with the practiced step of a craftsman, his fingers hovering over the spine.

"I'd know this tooling anywhere," he said, his voice carrying a grudging respect she'd never heard before. "Thomas Aldrich's work was... distinctive. The way he handled the morocco leather, the precision of these lines." His finger traced the gilt pattern without touching it. "I competed with him for years, tried to replicate his technique. Never quite managed it."

Meredith's throat tightened as she watched Harrison examine her father's last creation. The sunlight caught the gold tooling, highlighting the intricate pattern she'd watched her father design countless times at his workbench.

"This volume alone would have fetched thirty pounds at auction," Harrison continued, looking up at Lady Catherine. "The Carter commission was prestigious — only the finest bookbinders were even considered. Thomas Aldrich's reputation for excellence made him the natural choice."

Harrison's weathered hands traced the spine of her father's final work. The familiar gilt pattern caught the afternoon light, each line and curve telling a story of dedication she knew by heart.

"The Carters," Harrison continued, his voice carrying across the hushed drawing room, "their father passed before settling accounts. The widow, overwhelmed by mounting debts, sold the entire collection through Pembroke's Auction House." He glanced at Meredith, something softening in his usual stern expression. "Your father completed fifteen volumes before..." His words trailed off.

Lady Catherine's grip on her leather folder loosened slightly. "The books passed through several hands," Harrison explained, straightening his waistcoat. "First to a private collector in Bath, then to the Sheffield Literary Society. Lord Thornfield acquired them at the Bromley estate sale last year."

Martha's sharp intake of breath matched the ripple of murmurs through the assembled servants. Mrs Graves stepped forward, her usual stern demeanour cracking as she studied the book on the table.

"I remember that sale," she said, her voice unusually gentle. "His Lordship spent hours examining each volume, particularly taken with the craftsmanship of these specific pieces."

Harrison nodded, running a calloused finger along the edge of the morocco binding. "Thomas Aldrich's work was unmistakable. The way he treated the leather, his choice of tools — no other bindery in London could match it. These volumes represent the pinnacle of his craft, completed even as his health failed."

The room's atmosphere shifted palpably. The servants who had been avoiding Meredith's gaze now looked at her with dawning understanding. Even Lady Catherine's rigid posture softened slightly as she processed the connection between the prized books in her brother's library and the young maid standing before her.

Lady Catherine's fingers drummed against the leather folder, her composure wavering as the room's atmosphere shifted. "A few well-crafted books hardly

excuse—"

"If I may, Mother." Philip's voice cut through his mother's protest. He stepped forward, his shoulders squared with determination. "These books represent more than craftsmanship — they show dedication passed from father to daughter." His eyes met Meredith's, warm and unwavering. "I've witnessed that same dedication in Meredith's work, in my discussions with her, in her care for Alice."

He crossed the room to where Alice still trembled in the doorway. Offering his arm for support, he guided his cousin towards Meredith. Alice's bare feet made no sound on the carpet as she moved, her nightdress trailing behind her like a ghost's shroud.

"The value of family legacy isn't just in the books we preserve," Philip continued, his voice steady as he positioned himself beside Meredith. "It's in the knowledge we pass down, the care we show for others, the principles we uphold."

Alice's thin fingers found Meredith's hand and squeezed. The touch anchored Meredith as she stood between them — Philip's solid presence on one side, Alice's fierce loyalty on the other. The servants' earlier whispers had transformed into murmurs of approval.

Lady Catherine's lips pressed into a thin line as she surveyed the scene before her. The folder in her hands seemed to have lost its power, its damning contents overshadowed by the living testimony of those gathered. Mrs Graves nodded almost imperceptibly, and Martha beamed from her position among the staff.

"The Aldrich name," Philip said, his voice carrying across the now-quiet room, "stands for excellence in craft and character. Meredith honours that legacy every day through her actions here at Thornfield."

Meredith's hands trembled as she stood between Philip and Alice, their presence anchoring her amid the storm of revelations. Her heart thundered against her ribs as she absorbed the weight of Dr Bennett's testimony and Mr Harrison's unexpected defence.

The drawing room, that had moments ago, felt like a courtroom now hummed with shifting allegiances. Martha's steady presence, Mrs Graves's softening expression, and the murmurs of support from the staff she'd worked alongside these past months wrapped around her like a protective cloak.

From street urchin to valued member of the household — the journey stretched before her mind's eye like pages of a beloved book. She thought of Tommy's lessons in survival, now transformed into strength that helped her stand tall before Lady Catherine's accusations. Her father's tools upstairs weren't just instruments of craft anymore, but bridges between her past and present.

The room fell silent as Lord Thornfield rose from his chair. His tall frame cast a long shadow across the carpet as he stepped forward, his eyes moving deliberately between his sister's rigid posture and Meredith's upturned face. The weight of his impending words pressed against the air, and Meredith felt Alice's fingers tighten around hers.

Lord Thornfield cleared his throat, his expression grave as he surveyed the assembled household. The leather folder in Lady Catherine's hands seemed to mock them all as they waited, the future of Thornfield Hall balanced as precariously as a freshly bound book spine.

Through her racing heart, Meredith felt something new taking root — not the desperate hope of a street child seeking shelter, but the quiet confidence of someone who had found her place. Alice's warmth at her side, Philip's steady presence, and the chorus of supporters around her gave her strength to face whatever judgment came next.

46
RESOLVE

Lord Thornfield's stern expression softened, his eyes drifting to Charlotte's portrait above the mantle. The flickering candlelight caught the gilt frame, casting a warm glow across his late wife's gentle smile.

"Catherine." His voice carried the weight of memory. "Do you remember how our parents opposed my marriage to Charlotte? A gentleman's daughter working as a governess — they called it beneath our station."

Lady Catherine's fingers tightened around the leather folder. "That was different, Edmund. This girl—"

"Has shown the same spirit Charlotte possessed." Lord Thornfield's gaze settled on Meredith. "The courage to pursue what matters, regardless of circumstance. Charlotte saw worth in unexpected places. She taught me to do the same."

He crossed to his desk, running his fingers along the spine of the repaired King James Bible — Meredith's first work at Thornfield. "Your investigation was thorough, sister, and I appreciate your desire to protect our family. But just as I chose Charlotte, Philip must be free to make his own choices."

Lady Catherine's face flushed. "You cannot possibly—"

"I've made my decision." Lord Thornfield's tone held the quiet authority Meredith remembered from that first night in the library. "Meredith stays."

With a sharp intake of breath, Lady Catherine swept toward the door, her skirts rustling against the carpet. The folder dropped from her hands, scattering papers across the floor.

Lord Thornfield chuckled softly as the door slammed behind her. "Don't worry about Catherine," he said, turning to face the room. "She'll come around eventually. She always was the stubborn one of us siblings."

Alice rushed to her father, nearly stumbling in her haste. Her thin arms wrapped around his waist as she pressed her face into his coat. "Thank you, Papa. Thank you." Her voice cracked with emotion, and Lord Thornfield's hand came to rest on her head, gentle and protective.

Meredith's heart raced. The scattered papers at her feet contained her past — every painful detail of survival on London's streets laid bare. Yet Lord Thornfield had looked past it all, just as he had that first night in the library.

Her fingers found her mother's silver locket, drawing strength from its familiar weight. "Sir," she began, her voice barely above a whisper. The words caught in her throat as she met his eyes, seeing not judgment but understanding. "I cannot express my gratitude. You've shown me more kindness than I deserve."

"Nonsense," Lord Thornfield said, still holding Alice close. "You've earned your place here through your own merit. Charlotte would have done exactly the same."

The mention of his late wife made Meredith's chest tighten. She thought of her own mother, of evenings filled with

Shakespeare's words and the scent of leather bindings. Of second chances given freely, without condition.

"I won't disappoint your trust in me," Meredith said, meaning every word.

47
A NEW CHANCE

Meredith stood in Lord Thornfield's study as William and Susan Carter entered, their footsteps hesitant on the carpet. The siblings carried themselves with the bearing of their class, but their faces bore the weight of conscience. William's dark coat and Susan's navy dress spoke of mourning, though their father's passing had occurred years ago.

Lord Thornfield gestured for them to sit in the leather chairs before his desk. "Miss Aldrich, please join us."

Meredith's hands trembled slightly as she took her seat. These were the children of the man whose commission had consumed her father's final days. The unfinished volumes still haunted her dreams — her father bent over his workbench, hands bleeding as he raced against time.

"We've come to right a wrong," William said, his voice tight with emotion. He pulled out a folded document from his coat. "Our father commissioned twenty volumes from Thomas Aldrich. The work was nearly complete when—" He paused, swallowing hard.

Susan touched her brother's arm. "When our father fell ill," she continued. "It happened suddenly. Within a week, he was gone." Her fingers twisted in her lap. "Mother found herself drowning in debt. The creditors were relentless."

"The books," William's voice cracked. "Mother sold them through auction houses to pay the debts. She never honoured the contract with Mr Aldrich. We didn't know until we found Father's correspondence after her passing."

Meredith's throat constricted. She remembered the night she'd found her father slumped over the fifteenth volume, his precious bone folder still clutched in his lifeless hands. The Carter commission had killed him, yet here sat his client's children, carrying their own burden of grief and regret.

Susan wiped a tear from her cheek. "We cannot undo what was done, but we wish to make amends. It's what Father would have wanted."

Meredith's fingers found her mother's locket as William reached into his coat again. The familiar weight of silver against her palm steadied her racing heart.

"We've calculated the original commission price," William said, producing a leather-bound ledger. "Fifty pounds, with interest for the years passed."

The amount struck her like a physical blow. Fifty pounds. More money than her father had seen in his lifetime. More than 3 year's wages at Thornfield. She thought of the nights spent in St Michael's doorway, of Tommy sharing crusts of bread, of Mrs Cooper's quiet generosity.

Lord Thornfield's fingers drummed against his desk as he examined the ledger. The steady rhythm echoed through the study like a heartbeat. Meredith felt his gaze as he looked from the Carter siblings to her, measuring the moment's gravity.

"The craft deserves respect," William said, his voice firm despite its gentleness. "As does your father's memory." He placed a heavy envelope on the desk between them. "This can't undo the past, but perhaps it can help secure your future."

Meredith stared at the envelope, remembering her father's words about the commission securing her future. She hadn't understood then. The irony of it twisted in her chest — here was that security, delivered too late to save him, but perhaps in time to honour his final wish.

48
A NEW VENTURE

Meredith traced her fingers along the worn edge of her father's bone folder as she sat in Reverend Mills' study at St Michael's Church. The tools that had sustained her through the darkest nights now represented something greater — a chance to forge a different path for others.

"The school has space in the old carpenter's workshop," Reverend Mills said, adjusting his wire-rimmed spectacles. "With proper cleaning, it could house ten apprentices."

Her heart quickened at the possibility. "We could start with basic forwarding — teaching them to fold signatures, sew headbands." The memory of her father guiding her hands through these same motions filled her chest with warmth.

"The Carter payment would cover materials for at least a year." She pulled out the calculations she'd made the night before. "Thread, needles, paper, basic tools. Even some leather scraps from the tannery for practice."

Reverend Mills nodded, his eyes crinkling at her enthusiasm. "Many of these children have never held a book, let alone crafted one."

"That's why we must start with paper binding." Meredith spread her father's tools on the desk between them. "These techniques opened doors for me when I had nothing else. Each child should have their own basic kit — awl, needle, bone folder."

Meredith outlined her vision further. "They'll learn more than just a trade. It's about precision, patience, the satisfaction of creating something lasting." Her fingers brushed the silver locket at her throat. "My parents believed every book deserves care, just as every child deserves a chance."

"How many children did you have in mind?" Reverend Mills asked, reaching for his ledger.

"Eight to start. Small enough to provide individual attention." Meredith's mind raced with possibilities. "We could hold classes three afternoons a week, after their regular lessons."

～

MEREDITH STOOD before the gathered townspeople in St Michael's parish hall, her tools clasped tightly. The familiar weight steadied her nerves as she faced the sea of curious faces.

"Each child deserves the chance to create something lasting," she said, her voice growing stronger with each word. "My father taught me more than just binding books — he showed me the value of patience, precision, and pride in craftsmanship."

Mrs Cooper nodded from her seat in the front row, the baker's weathered hands folded in her lap. Next to her, Mr Cedar of the printing house leaned forward with interest.

"I propose we teach these skills to children who might otherwise never touch a book, let alone craft one." Meredith held up her father's tools, letting them catch the lamplight.

"With your support, we can provide them with the basic materials — paper, thread, simple tools."

Mr Harrison, the rival bookbinder who had recognised her father's work, raised his hand. "I have leather scraps from my workshop that could be used for practice. And I'd be willing to demonstrate advanced techniques once a month."

A murmur of approval rippled through the crowd. Other craftsmen began offering their own resources — Mr Cedar promised damaged sheets from his printing press, while the local carpenter volunteered to repair benches for the workspace.

Yet as Meredith discussed space requirements with the school board representative, doubt crept in. Could she really manage such an undertaking? The street child who once sold crude pamphlets for pennies, now proposing to teach others?

She caught Philip's encouraging smile from the doorway. His presence, along with the eager voices of the townspeople discussing possibilities, helped quiet the whispers of uncertainty.

49
NEW BEGINNINGS

Meredith's hands trembled as she arranged the last of the tools on the worn wooden workbench. Sunlight streamed through the windows of the makeshift classroom, catching dust motes that danced in the air.

Children filtered into the room, their footsteps hesitant on the creaking floorboards. Some wore patched clothes, others had shoes with holes, but their eyes sparkled with curiosity as they took in the neat rows of tools and stacks of paper.

The Carter payment had stretched far — new awls gleamed beside carefully cut lengths of thread, and squares of leather waited to be transformed. Each workstation held a bone folder, though not as fine as her father's treasured tool. Still, they would serve their purpose.

"Welcome," Meredith said, her voice steady despite her racing heart. "I'm Miss Aldrich, and today we begin our journey into the art of bookbinding." She moved among the children, learning their names — Matilda with her bright red hair, Johnathan whose fingers already showed the calluses of hard work, Joanie who clutched a tattered primer to her chest.

The weight of what she was attempting pressed down on her shoulders. These children looked to her with such trust, such hope. In their faces, she saw echoes of herself at their age, of Tommy who'd never had the chance to learn a trade, of all the children still struggling on London's unforgiving streets.

Meredith picked up a length of thread, holding it up to catch the light. "Every book tells two stories," she said. "The one written on its pages, and the one told by the hands that bound it together." The children leaned forward, drawn in by her words, their initial shyness melting away.

Standing before them, Meredith felt the presence of her father, the warmth of her mother's readings, the kindness of Mrs Cooper, the friendship of Tommy, the support of Lord Thornfield and Alice, the love of Philip — all of it flowing through her into this moment of new beginnings.

50
JOY IN THE CANDLELIGHT

WINTER, 1849

Snow fell in thick flakes outside the library windows of Thornfield Hall, coating the glass in delicate patterns of frost. Meredith breathed in the familiar scents of aged paper and fresh leather that filled her newly transformed sanctuary.

Philip sat across from her. "Tell me again about the first book you bound," he said, leaning forward in his chair.

"It was a collection of Shakespeare's sonnets." Meredith said wistfully. "Father let me choose the leather — this deep burgundy morocco that cost far too much for an apprentice's first attempt."

"And you ruined it completely, I expect?" Philip's smile held no judgment, only warmth.

"Three times over." Meredith laughed, the sound mixing with his own. "The leather tore, the glue leaked everywhere, and somehow I managed to sew the signatures in backward."

"Yet here you are, teaching others." His hand found hers across the space between them, warm and steady.

"Here we both are," she said softly, "defying expectations." The candlelight caught the silver of her mother's locket.

"My mother expected me to follow a very different path." Philip's thumb traced circles on her palm. "Oxford, ordination, a suitable marriage to some nobleman's daughter."

"Instead you spend your evenings discussing theology with a bookbinder's daughter."

"And I've never been happier." The conviction in his voice wrapped around her like a warm blanket against the winter chill.

Meredith watched Philip shift in his chair, his hand leaving hers as he reached inside his coat. His fingers trembled against the fabric, and she noticed a sheen of perspiration on his brow despite the winter chill seeping through the library windows.

"Meredith." His voice caught. He stood, then paced three steps away before turning back.

Her heart quickened. Philip's hazel eyes reflected both the candlelight and something deeper — a mixture of fear and determination she'd never seen before.

He reached into his coat pocket again, this time withdrawing a small box covered in dark velvet. The sight of it made her breath catch. Time seemed to slow as he lowered himself to one knee before her chair.

"My dearest Meredith." His fingers worked the box open, revealing a ring that captured and scattered the golden light. "You've shown me what true courage means — through your craft, your determination, your love of knowledge."

The ring sparkled, but Meredith found she couldn't look away from his eyes.

"I know we face obstacles. My mother, society's expectations..." He drew a steadying breath. "But I've never been more certain of anything than I am of this — of us. Will you marry me? Create a future where we can build something extraordinary together?"

Tears welled in Meredith's eyes, blurring the candlelight into golden stars. Her heart thundered against her ribs as she stared at the ring in Philip's trembling hands. This precious gift she'd never dared imagine possible during those cold nights in St Michael's doorway.

Her fingers found her silver locket, touching the cool metal that connected her to her past. She thought of her mother's gentle readings, her father's calloused hands teaching her to bind books, and how their love had given her the strength to survive when everything else was lost.

Philip knelt before her, patient and steady, his hazel eyes reflecting the same warmth they'd held during their first theological discussion between these towering shelves. He'd seen past her worn clothes and servant's position to the person beneath — the girl who could quote Augustine from memory and debate the merits of different binding techniques.

Her voice caught in her throat as memories flooded through her — Philip receiving her copy of 'The Tempest', their shared readings with Alice, his quiet support when Lady Catherine had tried to expose her past.

"Yes," Meredith breathed, the word carrying all the hope and love that filled her heart. "Yes, Philip."

The ring slipped onto her finger, cool metal warming against her skin. Through tear-filled eyes, she saw Philip's face transform with joy, his own eyes glistening in the candlelight.

51
UNITY

SPRING, 1850

Spring sunlight streamed through the school room's windows, casting warm patterns across the workbenches where a dozen young women bent over their tasks. Meredith moved between them, adjusting hands on bone folders and demonstrating the proper angle for folding signatures.

Lord Thornfield paused in the doorway, his expression softening as he watched the scene unfold. "Charlotte would have loved this," he murmured, catching Meredith's eye. "She always said books were meant to bring people together."

At the centre table, Alice sat with her shoulders straight, carefully marking spacing on a leather cover. Her cheeks held more colour these days, and the morning air from her brief garden walks had brought a healthy glow to her complexion. She had become determined to be well enough to attend Meredith's and Philip's wedding. "Father, come see what I've done," she called, holding up her work with steady hands.

The school room buzzed with quiet conversation and occasional bursts of laughter. Sarah Wilson, Tommy's sister, showed particular aptitude for gold tooling, while Martha's niece Ellen had mastered the art of sewing headbands. Even Mrs Graves had taken to attending these sessions, offering precise critiques of endpaper marbling techniques.

Sarah looked up, catching Meredith's gaze. Her eyes held none of the haunted shadows that had marked her brother's final days. Instead, they sparkled with pride as she lifted the cover to show her work.

"Is this right, Miss Aldrich?" Sarah presented the intricate pattern she'd created — roses and vines intertwining along the spine.

A lump formed in Meredith's throat. When Mr Pinkerton had first mentioned finding Tommy's sister, Meredith hadn't dared hope for such a perfect way to honour his memory. Yet here sat Sarah, transforming the same streets that had claimed her brother's life into art through the careful application of gilt and leather.

"It's beautiful," Meredith said, touching the still-warm tooling. "You have a natural eye for composition." She squeezed Sarah's shoulder, remembering how Tommy used to straighten his back whenever someone praised his quick hands or clever mind.

Sarah beamed at the compliment, then bent back to her work with renewed focus. The morning light caught the brass tools laid out before her – so different from the lock picks her brother had wielded, yet requiring that same delicate touch.

Through the window, Meredith glimpsed the spire of St Michael's where she and Tommy had once huddled in the doorway. The church bells rang out, marking another hour in this new life she'd built. But she carried the lessons of those desperate days with her still — in every book she bound, every skill she passed on, every chance she gave to children who reminded her of the friend who'd taught her to survive.

"Before we begin today's lesson," Meredith addressed the group, holding up her father's worn bone folder, "I want to share something with you. This tool belonged to my father, Thomas Aldrich. He taught me that every book tells two stories — the one written on its pages, and the one told through its binding."

The young women gathered closer, their faces eager and attentive. Some came from shops along Paternoster Row, others from St Michael's parish, and a few from grand houses where they served as maids. Yet here, united by craft and creativity, such distinctions faded away.

"When I lost everything," Meredith continued, "these tools and the skills my father taught me became my salvation. They opened doors I never thought possible." She smiled at her students, seeing in their eyes the same hunger for learning that had once burned in her own.

52
WEDDING PREPARATIONS

SUMMER, 1850

Meredith ran her fingers along the mahogany shelves of Thornfield's library, mapping out where the flowers would rest between the leather-bound volumes. The June morning light filtered through the glass, painting intricate patterns across Philip's sketches of their wedding layout.

"These roses should frame the window," Philip said, pointing to his detailed drawings. His sleeve brushed against her arm as he leaned over the plans.

Meredith adjusted a vase of sample blooms, positioning them where the wedding flowers would stand. Her mother's locket pressed cool against her skin, a constant reminder of those who couldn't be there.

The library hummed with preparation — Alice's careful arrangement of ribbons, Mrs Graves's meticulous polishing of the silver candlesticks, James's gentle organising of the ceremony space. Each person adding their own touch to the room that had first brought Meredith and Philip together.

Meredith watched Reverend Mills trace the worn spines of theological texts, his weathered hands moving with reverence across the leather bindings. The same hands that had offered her bread on bitter winter nights now held the prayer book for her wedding ceremony.

"This space holds such meaning for you both," he said, turning to face them. His eyes crinkled with warmth, the same gentle expression she remembered from those nights in St Michael's doorway.

Philip squeezed her hand. "We couldn't imagine being married anywhere else."

"You showed me kindness when I had nothing," Meredith said, her voice catching. "Having you perform the ceremony means everything."

Reverend Mills nodded, understanding flooding his features. He'd seen her transformation from a desperate child seeking shelter to the woman she'd become. "The Lord works in mysterious ways. Who would have thought that cold night would lead to this?"

The library around them buzzed with activity as Martha and Mrs Graves arranged flowers from the estate gardens — deep burgundy roses and delicate white lilies nestled between the shelves. Alice had insisted on picking the blooms herself, matching them to the rich wood tones of the bookcases.

"A small gathering," Meredith said, gesturing to the intimate space being prepared. "Just those who've meant the most to us."

James Blake had helped position the library's chairs to create a natural aisle between the towering shelves, leading to where she and Philip would exchange their vows beneath the largest window.

53
REFLECTIONS

Meredith stood before the mirror in her small chamber, the morning light catching the newly polished silver of her mother's locket. The intricate engravings had been restored to their original beauty, each curve and flourish telling its own story of craftsmanship and care.

Her fingers traced the delicate clasp Philip had commissioned the silversmith to repair. The metal felt cool against her skin as she remembered inheriting it that October morning, when her mother's presence had faded from their workshop forever. Now the tarnish had been lifted, revealing the subtle patterns she'd forgotten existed.

Opening the locket revealed the miniature portrait within — her mother and father on their wedding day, their faces bright with joy and promise. The image had been carefully cleaned, bringing back the vivid details that time had begun to blur. Elizabeth's gentle smile shone through, exactly as Meredith remembered from those afternoons of Shakespeare readings.

The restoration had been Philip's idea. He'd noticed how

she cradled the tarnished piece during their evening discussions in the library, understanding without words what it meant to her. The silversmith had worked miracles, breathing new life into the worn metal while preserving every precious memory it held.

Meredith lifted the chain over her head, letting the locket settle against her collarbone. In the mirror, she saw her mother's features reflected in her own — the same dark eyes that had watched over her first attempts at bookbinding, the same smile that had brightened their workshop on Paternoster Row. Though Elizabeth and Thomas were gone, their love remained, captured in this small silver heart that would accompany her down the aisle.

A soft knock pulled Meredith from her reflection. Lord Thornfield stood in the doorway, looking very sharp in his formal attire. The lines around his eyes crinkled with warmth as he regarded her.

"You look exactly as Charlotte did on our wedding day," he said, his voice catching. "That same light in your eyes. Your parents... If they could see you now."

Meredith smoothed her dress. "Thank you for standing in his place today."

"Your father would be proud of what you've accomplished here." Lord Thornfield stepped into the room. "The way you've transformed this household — Alice's renewed spirit, the children you teach, even Mrs Graves speaks of you with fondness now."

"I found my place here because you saw past my circumstances that night." Meredith touched the locket. "You gave me a chance when others wouldn't."

"You gave us far more in return." He offered his arm. "Shall we? Philip's waiting, and I believe Alice has arranged quite the surprise with the flowers."

Meredith slipped her hand into the crook of his elbow, feeling the sturdy support that had carried her through these past years. They descended the main staircase, their steps echoing in the morning quiet.

At the library entrance, Meredith paused. Through the heavy oak doors came the soft murmur of voices and the rustle of clothing. Lord Thornfield patted her hand.

"Ready?"

Meredith drew in a deep breath, touching the locket once more. She nodded.

The doors swung open, revealing the library transformed. Sunlight streamed through the stained glass, casting rainbow patterns across the gathered faces. Philip stood before the window, his smile bright as morning.

54
THE WEDDING

The library's familiar scent of leather and paper wrapped around Meredith as she and Lord Thornfield moved between the rows of books. Her father's bone folder, displayed on burgundy velvet near the window, caught the morning light. Philip's eyes never left her as she approached, his smile growing wider with each step.

Reverend Mills stood before the window, his weathered face bright with joy. The same man who had once shared soup with her in St Michael's doorway now raised his hands in blessing.

Alice beamed from her chair in the front row, her face flushed with happiness rather than fever. She had woven flowers through the book displays, their fragrance mixing with the familiar library air. Dr Bennett sat beside her, his kind eyes crinkling at the corners as he watched the ceremony unfold.

Mrs Cooper dabbed at her eyes with her apron, the same hands that had once left warm bread on their doorstep now clasped in delight. She had brought fresh-baked treats for after the ceremony, their sweet aroma drifting through the air.

The morning light streamed through the stained glass, casting coloured shadows across their joined hands as they exchanged rings. Each face in the gathering, reflected the journey that had brought them to this moment — from the streets of London to the heart of Thornfield's library.

Meredith's heart swelled as she caught sight of Sarah Wilson among the witnesses. Tommy's sister looked wonderful in her dove-grey dress, her eyes bright with unshed tears. The girl who had once learned basic forwarding techniques in Meredith's first class now carried herself with the confidence of a skilled craftswoman. Sarah's fingers, calloused from working with leather and thread, twisted a handkerchief as she watched the ceremony unfold.

A soft scratching sound drew Meredith's attention to Alice, who balanced a leather-bound sketchbook on her lap. Her friend's artistic talent, honed through long hours confined to her chambers, showed in every precise stroke of her pencil. Alice's hand moved with sure purpose across the page, capturing the play of light through the stained glass window and the way it painted rainbow patterns across the gathered assembly.

Alice's tongue poked out slightly as she concentrated, her eyes darting between the happy couple and her drawing. She sketched rapidly but carefully, determined to preserve every detail — the way Philip's eyes crinkled at the corners when he smiled, the delicate fall of Meredith's simple dress, and the proud set of Lord Thornfield's shoulders as he stood beside them.

The scratch of Alice's pencil provided a gentle counterpoint to Reverend Mills' words. Her keen artist's eye didn't miss a single detail — the worn spine of the Bible in the reverend's hands, the subtle patterns of shadow cast by the book-lined shelves, and the way Sarah Wilson clasped her hands together in joy as she watched her mentor's happiness unfold.

Meredith's heart thundered against her ribs as she turned to face Philip. His eyes met hers, warm and steady.

"I, Philip Ashworth, take you, Meredith Aldrich, to be my wife." His voice rang clear through the library's hushed atmosphere. "I vow to stand beside you through every challenge life presents, to cherish your brilliant mind and generous heart, and to support your dreams as you've supported mine. All the days of my life, I promise to be your partner in every endeavour."

At the back of the room, Lady Catherine stood straight-backed and proper, her lips pressed into a thin line. But as Philip spoke his vows, something in her expression shifted. The rigid set of her shoulders softened slightly, and her eyes lingered on her son's face, taking in his evident joy. Meredith caught the subtle change, recognising that while the path ahead might be long, there was hope for understanding to grow.

Meredith's fingers tightened around Philip's as she drew a steadying breath. "I, Meredith Aldrich, take you, Philip Ashworth, to be my husband." Though quiet, her voice carried the same conviction she'd felt when binding her first book. "I promise to walk beside you through joy and hardship, to share in your passions and support your aspirations, and to face whatever comes with the same courage that brought us here. I will be your constant companion, your trusted friend, and your loving wife until my last breath."

Reverend Mills stepped forward, his weathered face bright with joy. The same voice that had once offered comfort on cold nights now filled the library with warmth. "Love, like the books that surround us, tells many stories. Some chapters bring joy, others challenge us to grow stronger. But true love, like the binding that holds pages together, keeps us unified through every season."

He raised his hands in blessing. "May your union be strengthened by compassion, enriched by understanding, and guided by the values you both hold dear. Remember always the importance of community that brought you together, the faith that sustained you, and the courage that helped you overcome every obstacle."

Meredith's heart fluttered as Philip's lips met hers. The kiss, gentle and sweet, sealed their vows beneath the library's vaulted ceiling. Sunlight streamed through St Jerome's image in the stained glass, washing them in jewel-toned rays of amber, sapphire, and ruby.

Applause burst through the hushed silence. The sound bounced between the towering shelves, multiplying until it felt like the whole of London celebrated with them. Martha's enthusiastic clapping mixed with Mrs Cooper's joyful sobs. Dr Bennett's dignified applause blended with James Blake's hearty approval.

Alice's sketch pencil clattered to the floor as she joined the celebration, her usually pale cheeks flushed with happiness. Lord Thornfield stood tall beside her chair, his stern features softened by a smile that reminded Meredith of the night he'd discovered her repairing a Bible by moonlight.

Sarah's eyes shone with tears as she cheered, her craftsman's hands still bearing traces of gold leaf from her morning's work. Even Mrs Graves, who had once viewed Meredith with such suspicion, dabbed at her eyes with a handkerchief while trying to maintain her usual composure.

The library, which had first sheltered Meredith on that bitter winter night, now held all the people who had transformed her life. From the streets of London to this moment, each person gathered had played a part in her journey. Their joy echoed off the leather-bound spines that lined the walls, filling the space with warmth that rivalled the coloured light dancing around them.

Philip squeezed her hand, his touch grounding her in the moment. The same fingers that had traced theological arguments and poetry now intertwined with hers, promising a future built on their shared love of literature and learning.

Alice quickly picked up her pencil and made a final touch, her eyes bright as she studied her completed work. The sketch captured more than just the ceremony – it held the essence of their shared journey. Each carefully rendered detail spoke volumes: the worn spine of the King James Bible Meredith had first repaired, the bone folder displayed on burgundy velvet, and the way the morning light streamed through St Jerome's window.

Her skilled hand had caught the tender way Philip gazed at Meredith, the proud set of Lord Thornfield's shoulders, and the joy radiating from every face in attendance. Even Lady Catherine's softening expression found its way onto the page, testament to Alice's keen eye for detail.

"Meredith, Philip," Alice called softly, her voice steady despite her usual frailty. She lifted the leather-bound sketchbook with delicate fingers. "I want you to have this."

The newly married couple moved closer as Alice held out her work. The page seemed to breathe with life — each pencil stroke conveying the warmth and intimacy of the moment.

Meredith's heart caught at the sight. There in graphite and shadow lay everything that mattered: the library that had given her shelter, the friends who had become family, and the love that had bloomed among the books. Alice's gift preserved not just their wedding day, but the culmination of all their shared struggles and triumphs.

"Alice, it's beautiful," Meredith whispered, taking in how

her friend had rendered the rainbow light falling across the gathering. The sketch held the same careful attention to detail that Meredith brought to her bookbinding – each line placed with purpose and care.

Philip leaned closer, his shoulder brushing Meredith's as they studied the drawing together. "You've captured everything perfectly," he said, his voice thick with emotion.

The library transformed as servants wheeled in tables draped with crisp linens. Mrs Cooper's pastries sat alongside Martha's roasted chicken and potatoes, their mingled aromas filling the air. Silver platters gleamed with delicacies from the Thornfield kitchen, while crystal decanters caught the colored light from the stained glass.

Meredith's heart swelled as she watched Mrs Cooper arrange her famous meat pies beside a towering display of fruit tarts. The same hands that had once left food on their doorstep now served generous portions to each guest, her eyes twinkling with pride.

"These are the same pies that kept your father going," Mrs Cooper whispered, pressing an extra slice into Meredith's hands. The familiar taste brought tears to her eyes — memories of kindness during darker days.

Dr Bennett raised his glass, his kind face flushed with happiness. "To Meredith and Philip – may their love continue to challenge our assumptions and brighten our days." The toast rang through the library, echoed by the gathered company.

James Blake clinked his glass against Lord Thornfield's. "Who would have thought that catching a young bookbinder at midnight would lead to this?" His face creased with joy as servants passed between the guests with trays of champagne.

Sarah approached with a small package wrapped in brown paper. "From all your students," she said, her voice trembling slightly. Inside lay a collection of hand-bound volumes, each spine tooled with golden roses — the signature design she'd perfected under Meredith's guidance.

Martha wove through the crowd distributing plates, pausing often to embrace friends and share in their joy. Even Mrs Graves unbent enough to smile.

The library buzzed with conversation and laughter, the sound bouncing off leather-bound spines and dancing between the towering shelves. Everywhere Meredith looked, she saw faces that had played a part in her journey.

55
OUR NEXT CHAPTER

Meredith stepped into the afternoon air, Philip's hand warm in hers. They had decided to take a quiet moment together away from the library, though muffled cheerful voices could still be heard within. Summer breeze lifted loose strands of her hair, carrying the scent of roses from the garden below.

Her mother's locket pressed cool against her skin, a familiar comfort as she gazed across the manor grounds. Sunlight caught the fresh gilt edges of Sarah's bound volumes tucked under her arm, sparking like captured stars.

Philip squeezed her hand. "I never thought breaking into a library could lead to this."

"Neither did I." Meredith traced her thumb over his ring, the metal still foreign and wonderful against her skin. "Though I suppose books have always had a way of changing lives."

They stood in comfortable silence, watching shadows dance across the lawn. The same breeze that had once whipped through her thin clothes on London's streets now wrapped around them like a gentle embrace, carrying the distant sound of birdsong and the rustle of leaves.

Philip drew her closer, his shoulder pressing against hers. The warmth of him grounded her in this moment — no longer the desperate girl seeking shelter, nor the maid hiding her past, but simply herself, complete and accepted.

"Ready for our next chapter?" His voice held all the quiet joy she felt bubbling in her chest.

Meredith nodded, her heart full as she looked up at him. The afternoon sun painted everything in soft gold, transforming the world around them into something new and precious.

Together they breathed in the fresh air, letting it fill their lungs with possibility. Their joined hands formed a bridge between who they had been and who they would become — two people who had found each other among the books, ready to write their own story.

THE FIRST CHAPTER OF 'THE ORPHAN'S RESCUED NIECE'

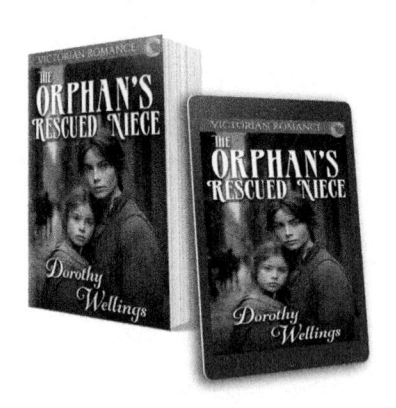

SOUTHWARK, LONDON, 1871

Beatrice Portly sat at the edge of the damp, mould-infested pavement waiting for her brother, Roy, who told her to not go anywhere otherwise he'd not be able to find her. Her brown shoes had thinned at the soles and water seeped between her toes as she kicked at the small puddles gathered in the potholes of Theed Street. She pulled her worn-out woollen coat to cover her nose. The smelly, unpleasant air was worse as the gutsy wind blew everything hither and thither in its path.

Oblivious to the wind, children from the neighbourhood laughed and kicked cans down the street, others built castles out of pebbles and rubble. Above the street, women were sharing stories as they hung wet clothes on ropes between the tenements. People had set up broken and chipped tables and chairs on the dire pavement in hopes of selling their wares.

Across the street, a middle-aged woman welcomed a man and a young boy covered in soot inside their house. She imagined it would be the same as their block. The five-story building with four tiny flats on each floor bulked with varied-sized families. She and Roy shared one room, Auntie Sadie slept on a cot in the corner of the living room cum kitchen, which had a table, three chairs and a cast iron stove with a grate.

"Hoi, why you sticking your feet in the water?"

Roy's croaky voice jammed in her ear as he sat beside her. His faded blue coat was thicker than when he'd left her earlier and his loosely-fitted cap was askew over his left ear.

"I'm bored. You were gone for hours," Beatrice said with a huff. "Next time I want to go with you."

"No, you can't."

"You always say that."

"It's 'cause you'll just get in the way."

"In the way of what?"

He grabbed her arm and pulled her to her feet. "Let's get home before Auntie Sadie does. She'll be in a dander if we're not there."

Beatrice side-glanced her brother with annoyance and noticed a shine inside his coat. She opened her mouth but knew better and said nothing. Roy grasped her hand and sprinted to the end of the street, squirming between narrow alleys until they crossed the Southwark Bridge over the dark, murky Thames River.

"Slow down," Beatrice said pulling her hand from her brother's grasp and said, "I can't run fast like you." She stopped and leaned over placing her palms over her knees, panting. Her mop hat fell to her soggy feet amidst the mushy ground and she seized it with a sigh. Aunt Sadie would reprimand her as she had cleaned it only yesterday.

"We're almost there, see?" Roy said, pointing to his left. "Down Park Street, turn a few corners and then we're in Red Cross. It's not far."

"For you," said Beatrice between breaths, covering her head with the soiled hat. "Lant Street is far."

"Don't dally. Auntie Sadie is coming through Piccadilly so we don't have much time."

"I wanted to go to school," Beatrice said lifting her chin with a scowl on her face. "What do you think she's gonna say when I tell her I didn't go."

"Nothing, you say nothing, but a fine day."

Roy snapped her hand into his and dragged her behind him slipping past stationery wagons and with the slight of his hand grabbed whatever he could as they passed merchants. Those who saw him were too late and offered words of obscenity waving angry fists in the air.

"Take this," he said, shoving a hunk of dry bread into her hand as they snuck into an alleyway.

Beatrice's stomach growled. She hadn't eaten all day. Though she knew where he got the bread from, she took it and guilt filled her as she ate it.

"Now hurry, let's go," Roy urged, tugging on her arm. "Please, Bea, you know Auntie Sadie gets home early when she works in Piccadilly."

With a massive nod and not wanting to disappoint her brother, she said, "Yes, let's go, Roy."

She grabbed hold of his hand and they scurried through the streets and arrived home just as Auntie Sadie ambled around the corner, her large shoulder strap bag dangling from her shoulder.

"Put on the stove, quick!" Beatrice yelled, stomping up the whittled staircase behind her brother to the third floor. "I'll peel potatoes."

Behind one of the doors adjacent to them, a baby wailed.

The door rattled as Roy pushed the door open and he stumbled over the rutted floor. While Beatrice hurried to the tiny box in the corner of the larder where they kept a table, Roy grabbed the flint on the floor near the stove and within minutes a soft glow radiated from it.

Rubbing their hands they heard the door creak open followed by shuffling. Beatrice bolted to the table and picked up a knife, her heart thumped. Would Auntie Sadie know? Grown-ups had a way of knowing things. Her mind raced thinking of what to tell her aunt.

Auntie Sadie limped into the living room where Roy greeted her at the door, took the bag from her and placed it onto her cot.

"Did you have a good day?" Auntie Sadie said with a smile in her voice, sitting on a wobbly back-slated chair that Roy had placed near the grate for her.

"Oh yes," Roy answered with a bright grin.

"Must I chop the potatoes?" Beatrice said from the minuscule larder, and she saw her aunt nod through the gaps between the rotting timeworn boards of wood. Auntie's eyes were droopy and her face weary.

"Why don't you rest," Roy offered. "I'll get more water and help Bea cook supper."

"Helpful today, aren't you?" Auntie Sadie said with a raised brow. She kicked off her shoes and slid the chair forward toward the grate. "Makes me think you're up to no good again."

Roy's face drained of colour and his eyes widened in mock horror. "No, I'm gonna get more water and..." his voice dropped, but added a hint of cheer, "I got some vegetables and fruit. They aren't too fresh, but we can boil them."

Auntie Sadie's brows knitted. "You went to the market again, didn't you?"

When Roy remained silent and his eyes hit the floor, Auntie Sadie clicked her tongue with disdain.

"Why do you think I work extra days cleaning houses?" she said in a warbled voice. "To get us by, that's why. Do you want the bobbies to take you to the workhouse?"

Roy shook his head and stared at her, "No, I don't want that. I only want to help."

"I don't want Roy to go to the workhouse," Beatrice said, tears pricking her eyes. "We'll never see each other."

"Then go to school," Auntie Sadie peered at them both. "You didn't go to school, did you?" she glared at Beatrice, who shook her head.

"I'm sorry, I'll go tomorrow. I promise." Beatrice's heart thumped harder. "Please don't send Roy away, he's not thirteen yet, he can still come to school."

Auntie Sadie turned away and stared at the warm, flickering glow with a sigh. "I don't want either of you to go there. It's not good for families to be split up." Pointing at her bag she said, "Look inside. The Hembley's have thrown out clothes and shoes. There's an old dress and shoes for you, Beatrice, throw out the ones you have now. Trousers and a shirt for you, Roy."

Beatrice and Roy stared at each other in delight and whooped.

"Thank you, thank you," said Beatrice rushing towards their auntie's bag with Roy close behind her.

"Stop, Roy," Auntie Sadie said, glaring at him. "Fetch the water first. Think twice before leaving your sister alone and now I have to wash her hat again."

Roy's lips tipped downward and his head bobbed. "I'm sorry," he whispered and grabbed the pail before disappearing out the door.

Pain stabbed Beatrice's heart staring after him as she held onto the new dress, well, old, but it had no holes. She knew he meant well, but she wished her brother would listen. Roy, like many children, would steal and Auntie Sadie scolded him whenever she found out.

Beatrice pulled out two small black-heeled shoes. "Aunt Sadie, why do rich people throw out such nice things?" She inspected the shoes and decided they only needed a polish to shine.

Aunt Sadie rose to her feet. "Take off those shoes and dry your feet. You'll get sick. People get tired of the same clothes and want to look new and different."

"Would I look different in this new dress?" Beatrice said, holding up the dress to her shoulders, the hem stopped at her ankles.

Removing the grubby mop hat from Beatrice's head, Auntie Sadie planted a kiss on her head and said, "No, you're still pretty as you. You can't be anyone, but you. Go dry your feet and I'll take over supper."

Exaggerated *oofs* and *ah's* sounded from the door and Beatrice turned to her aunt giggling. She ran to the door and shifted it open for Roy staggering under the hefty weight of the pail, water spilling everywhere.

"Leave it by the door," Auntie Sadie said with a jerk of her head. "Try on the shirt and trousers, you're going to need them soon."

"What do you mean?" he said, digging inside her bag and pulling out brown trousers and a white cotton shirt with buttons.

"I'll tell you later," Auntie Sadie said.

"These are fancy, a bit big though. I'll grow into them, thank you."

Auntie Sadie walked to the pail of water and filled a pot to boil the potatoes. Turning to Roy she said, "Hand me those vegetables. You both look like waifs. We'll make do with the vegetables and have the fruit after supper."

Roy's face beamed and he dropped the clothes onto the cot. He dug into his coat and like a magician, he pulled out carrots and beans.

The Hembly's cook took a liking to Auntie Sadie and whenever there were leftovers, she shared them. Auntie Sadie had never looked happier announcing there'd be meat in the broth. She'd been given extra money and had bought fresh bread. Despite Auntie Sadie's disapproval, after supper, they'd enjoyed the apples and bananas Roy had provided.

With the candle burning on the stool in the living room, Beatrice loved hearing stories about the rich people and how they lived. Auntie Sadie told it like it was a fairytale. A house with rooms the size of their tenement and larger didn't sound real.

Auntie Sadie yawned and kissed them both on their cheeks. "I'll be going to sleep now. It's an early start to get to the Richardson House in Hyde Park. Don't stay up too late."

Once Auntie Sadie had gone to bed, Roy tapped Beatrice's hand and shoved something cool into her hand.

"Happy birthday," he said with a shy grin. "I'm sorry I

couldn't get anything for you last week, but I couldn't find anything you'd like. You're nine now, practically a lady."

Beatrice's eyes widened with astonishment. Glancing from her brother to her hand, she was breathless. He'd given her a shiny brass bracelet in her hand with green, white, gold and pink beads.

"See, the green is like your eyes," his grin broadened, "the light pink is your hair. There are nine gold beads."

"Thank you," Beatrice stammered, choking over her words. It was the most beautiful thing she'd ever seen. "I love it, but-but I can't keep this." She held it out to him. "Auntie Sadie would be angry if she knew."

His face turned solemn and he wrapped his hand over hers, pushing her hand back. "It's yours. You can't give away a present now, can you?"

"No, you're right," she said, shaking her head and tears gathered in her eyes. Leaning forward she embraced him. "I won't show Auntie Sadie. I'll keep it safe."

"Good," his bright grin returned. "Go sleep now. I need to meet up with some friends."

"But...it's night-time and—"

"Shush, Bea, you'll wake Auntie Sadie," he said covering her mouth with his forefinger. "I won't be late, promise. Go sleep now."

He hopped to his feet and gripped his coat, before hurrying out the door.

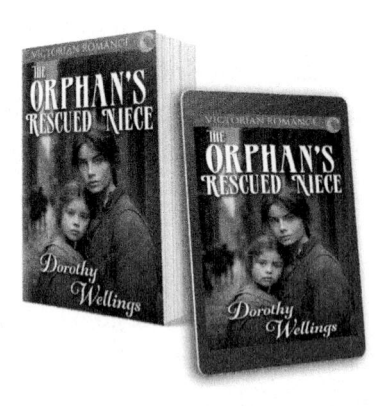

**Click here to read the rest of
'The Orphan's Rescued Niece'**

A tale of family, sacrifice, and the courage to choose a better future.

BEATRICE PORTLY's life has been one of constant struggle and sacrifice. Orphaned at a young age, she and her brother Roy are raised by their kind-hearted Aunt Sadie in the unforgiving slums of Victorian London. As Beatrice grows from a wide-eyed child into a resilient young woman, she finds herself caught between her love for her troubled brother and her desire for a life free from poverty and fear.

When Roy's drinking spirals out of control, threatening not only himself but also his young daughter Sadie, Beatrice is forced to make an impossible choice. With the help of the compassionate Oscar Talloway, a man from a world far removed from her own, Beatrice must find the strength to forge a new path - not just for herself, but for her beloved niece as well.

As the shadows of her past threaten to engulf her, Beatrice

discovers that sometimes the bravest thing one can do is to let go. Will she have the courage to break free from the cycle of poverty and addiction that has defined her life? And in doing so, can she open her heart to the possibility of love and a future she never dared to imagine?

'The Orphan's Rescued Niece'

OUR GIFT TO YOU

AS A WAY TO SAY THANK YOU WE WOULD LOVE TO SEND YOU THIS BEAUTIFUL STORY FREE OF CHARGE.

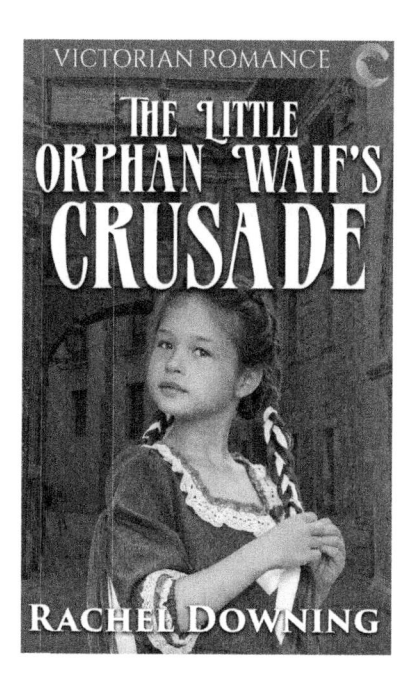

Click here for your FREE COPY of

'The Little Orphan Waif's Crusade'

CornerstoneTales.com/sign-up

In the wake of her father's passing, seven-year-old Matilda is determined to heal her sister Effie's shattered spirit.

Desperate to restore joy to Effie's life, Matilda embarks on a daring quest, aided by the gentle-hearted postman, Philip. Together, they weave a plan to ignite the flame of love in Effie's heart once more.

At Cornerstone Tales we publish books you can trust. Great tales without sex or swearing, but with all of the mystery and romance you expect from a great story.

Be the first to know when we release new books, take part in our fun competitions, and get surprise free books in your inbox by signing up to our free VIP Reader list.

As a thank you you'll receive a copy of 'The Little Orphan Waif's Crusade' by *Rachel Downing* straight away, alongside other gifts.

Click here to sign up for our mailing list, and receive your FREE stories.

CornerstoneTales.com/sign-up

LOVE VICTORIAN ROMANCE?

Another Dorothy Welling's Victorian Romance

The Moral Maid's Unjust Trial

Matilda must fend for herself when her father is wrongfully accused for a crime he didn't commit.

Get 'The Moral Maid's Unjust Trial' Here!

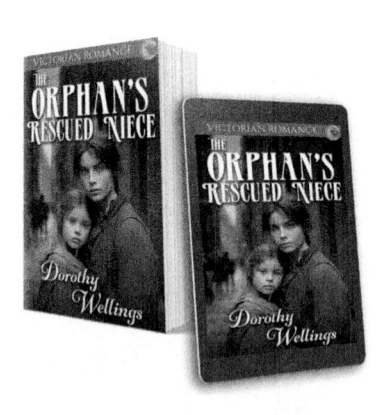

The Orphan's Rescued Niece

As Beatrice grows from a wide-eyed child into a resilient young woman, she finds herself caught between her love for her troubled brother and her desire for a life free from poverty and fear.

Get 'The Orphan's Rescued Niece' Here!

Books by our other Victorian Romance Writer *RACHEL DOWNING*

Two Steadfast Orphan's Dreams

Follow the stories of Isabella and Ada as they overcome all odds and find love.

Get 'Two Steadfast Orphan's Dreams' Here!

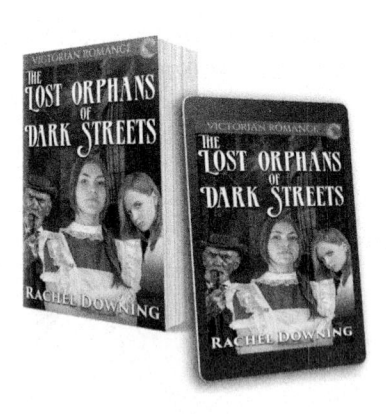

The Lost Orphans of Dark Streets

Follow the stories of Elizabeth and Molly as they negotiate the dangerous slums and find their place in the world.

Get 'The Lost Orphans of Dark Streets' Here!

The Orphan Prodigy's Stolen Tale

When ten-year-old Isabella Farmerson's world shatters with the tragic loss of her parents, she's thrust into a life of hardship and uncertainty.

Get 'The Orphan Prodigy's Stolen Tale' Here!

The Workhouse Orphan Rivals

Childhood sweethearts torn apart. A promise broken. A love that refuses to die.

Get 'The Workhouse Orphan Rivals' Here!

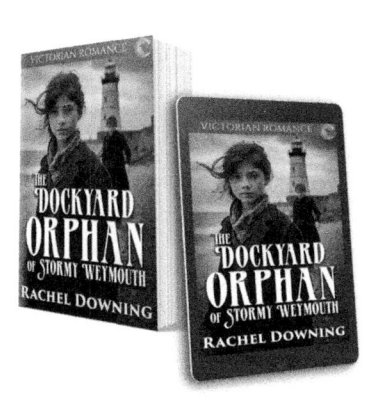

The Dockyard Orphan of Stormy Weymouth

Sarah Campbell's world crumbles when a tragic accident claims her parents' lives. She finds solace in the lighthouse's beam that guides ships to safety. But it's a young fisherman wrestling with his own loss, who truly captures her heart.

Get 'The Dockyard Orphan of Stormy Weymouth' Here!

The Orphan's Christmas Hymn

Seven-year-old Clara Winters' world shatters when tragedy strikes days before Christmas. Sent to St. Mary's Church Orphanage, she finds her only solace in the hymns that once filled her happy home. When her angelic voice catches the attention of the kind-hearted Reverend Thornton and his musically gifted son Edward, Clara dares to dream of a brighter future.

Get 'The Orphan's Christmas Hymn' Here!

The Workhouse Orphan's Redemption

In the brutal world of Victorian London, Emma Redbrook's life begins in tragedy. Orphaned and trapped in Grimshaw's Workhouse, she endures cruelty that would break most spirits. But Emma's unwavering faith becomes her beacon of hope — and her strength.

Get 'The Workhouse Orphan's Redemption' Here!

If you enjoyed this story, sign up to our mailing list to be the first to hear about our new releases and any sales and deals we have.

We also want to offer you a Victorian Romance novella - 'The Little Orphan Waif's Crusade' - absolutely free!

Click here to sign up for our mailing list, and receive your FREE stories.

CornerstoneTales.com/sign-up

Printed in Great Britain
by Amazon